Published by The Painted Chickadee Publishing Co.
of Burlington, Iowa
thepaintedchickadee.com

First published in 2020

ISBN 9780578793382

Printed in the United States of America

The Children of
Horseshoe Hideout

Rebecca Matthews Vorkapich

Dedicated to Natalie and Liam
for keeping my love of children's books alive.

Table of Contents

IN HOT WATER

Hannah was pretty sure there was no such thing as cooties. Even so, she was certain her aunt's bedroom was full of them.

It was laundry day, so she had to be there, but by now she had the routine down pat. She yanked the sheets from the bed and threw them in the basket, touching only what was necessary. She knew she would be done making the bed in four minutes, but more importantly, she would be done with this chore forever in a matter of weeks.

On the first Saturday of September in the quaint

river town of Flinthills, Iowa, *most* of the town was alive with fun-filled activity. The intense heat of summer was over so air conditioners ceased to hum and windows were thrown open to welcome the fresh air. Families packed picnics and loaded their boats to go fishing on the Mississippi. A record number of children swarmed the city pool for a final swim of the season. Those preferring dry land rode bikes to the park to play ball or to hike on Black Hawk trail.

But Hannah, Wes and Jamie Faris were not like most kids. No picnics, fishing or bike riding for them. Weekends meant an endless list of chores. The work began after school on Friday and ended—temporarily—when they trudged upstairs to their shared attic bedroom for the night.

Hannah took one last look around Aunt Olga's bedroom. Satisfied that she had gathered all the laundry, she picked up the basket and headed for the door. She glanced out the hallway window at the clear blue sky—a cerulean blue—maybe mixed with a little cobalt. She loved to imagine the colors she would use to paint a scene, especially since she rarely had time to paint anymore.

She spotted Wes pushing the mower through the weeds. At nine, Wes was younger than her by two years, and though it wasn't his fault, goats would do just as well on the yard. Aunt Olga didn't care that her yard was a shambles. She had Wes keep it mowed so the neighbors wouldn't come knocking at her door to complain. She didn't want anyone knocking at her door. Still, Hannah wouldn't mind switching chores with Wes sometime. *At least he was outside—even if he wasn't playing. Never playing.*

Hannah let her mind wander, as she often did. She imagined herself outside playing with her best friend, Annie. They loved playing tetherball at recess or just walking around the playground talking about favorite classes, teachers and books. Annie was the only friend that knew more than a little about Hannah's circumstances. For example, she knew Hannah would never be allowed to go to her house, so she finally quit inviting her. Hannah was careful not to say too much, and grateful that Annie had learned not to pry.

A loud, cawing crow flew by the window and startled Hannah out of her daydream. Olga had never allowed her or her brothers to accept an invitation from a friend. "No, you're not going to anybody's house," she said. "And they aren't welcome here." Hannah could feel her nose turning red and her eyes starting to burn. Even though she and her brothers would soon be free of Olga, she still wouldn't be able to spend time with Annie…maybe ever.

3

It had been two years since the Faris children had lost their parents in a tragic accident. Hannah's memories of the days that followed were a blur, except for one thing: they had been taken from a loving home and thrown into the middle of, well, that would be a bad word. Instead of open arms and a sympathetic heart, Aunt Olga had met them at the door with a beady-eyed stare, a broom, and a dustpan.

"Go clean the attic. That's your room and I don't want you tracking any dirt down here. You go outside to mow the lawn, shovel snow or to bring in the groceries. Not to *play*." She said 'play' like she'd just swallowed overcooked okra. "You eat what I tell you and when I tell you. Bath night is Sunday, but you're not to turn on the hot water. It's expensive and will make you lazy. There's too much work to be done to spend time lingering in a hot bath. If you disobey my rules, there will be consequences!"

From that point forward, they secretly called her Aunt Ogre. Hannah and Wes suffered the worst of the consequences, but even Jamie—had been forced to miss dinner many times. His biggest crime was trying to play with Olga's collection of breakable cats, but his most frequent crime was climbing the pantry shelves in search of her secret stash of sweets. Even so, Olga had never struck Jamie for his rule-breaking. Hannah was puzzled by this behavior of Olga's, but she was also grateful…while it lasted.

Hannah and Wes weren't so lucky. Olga had a knack for striking with enough force to cause pain but without leaving any serious bruises behind which might alert teachers or neighbors to her actions. For Hannah, the physical punishments weren't the worst. It was seeing her brothers hurt that caused her the most pain.

Hannah recalled a Sunday night just a few weeks past. It was time for Jamie's bath. He was still recovering from a lingering cough. Hannah felt bad sticking him in the cold bath water, but he needed to be clean for school, so she couldn't put it off any longer. Jamie started to shiver before he stepped into the tub. Hannah couldn't bear it.

"Jamie, don't get in yet," she whispered. "I'm going to add some hot water, but we can't tell, ok?"

"K," he said, still sounding like a frog.

Hannah turned the knob for the hot water and nearly jumped out of her skin. The pipe vibrated with such a loud clanking, she was sure it would break through the wall. "Oh no," she said as she quickly turned it off. She looked toward the door, fearful the sound may have carried downstairs.

As if on cue, Olga's recliner slammed shut. Then came the dreaded thaDUMP, thaDUMP as Olga limped to the bottom of the stairs. Hannah felt the hair rise on the back of her neck.

Then, "Who in the Sam Hill turned on the hot water up there? Get down here now!"

ENOUGH IS ENOUGH

Hannah wrapped Jamie in a towel. "Wait here," she said.

"Don't go down there, Hannah," Jamie croaked.

Hannah gave a weak smile. "It'll be ok." She hurried downstairs, spilling out her story before she reached the bottom step.

"Aunt Olga, I'm worried about Jamie's cough and he…"

Olga stomped her foot then stepped within inches of Hannah. There was no escaping her foul breath.

"You know the rule!"

Hannah scrunched her face to brace for the expected slap, but the pain she felt was at her wrist. She opened her eyes to find her treasured bracelet in Olga's hand.

Hannah gasped. "No! You broke it!" She rubbed the welt forming on her wrist where the silver chain once rested, then reached out to take it back. "Mom and Dad gave me that."

Olga held the bracelet out of Hannah's reach.

"Olga, please. I'm sorry I disobeyed you, but I did it for Jamie. He should have gone to a doctor. Don't you care that he…"

Hannah was interrupted by her brother's loud croaking from the top of the stairs. "Give it back to Hannah, you stealer! Or I'm callin' the cops!" Jamie finished his threat by sticking out his tongue and bolting for the bathroom.

"Get him down here," Olga ordered.

"Why? I turned on the hot water."

"Don't question me, girl. Get him down here now. Do you want this bracelet back or not?"

Hannah hesitated, but only for a second. "But it was my idea. Why do you want him?"

Hannah jumped backwards as Olga roared, "Get down here this instant young man, or I'm coming for you!"

"Keep the bracelet," Hannah said. She ran up the stairs, pulled Jamie from the bathroom and sent him to the attic. In two years, Hannah had never seen Olga attempt the stairs. Jamie would be safe in the attic and hopefully Olga would cool off.

But the bracelet was gone and Hannah was heartbroken. When they all retreated to the attic that night, it was Jamie who blurted out the details of the story to Wes. "I told her I was going to call the cops on her and that's what we should do," he suggested.

Hannah finally spoke. "We've been through this before, Jamie. We can't tell anyone, remember? Especially not the police. Like Olga says, if we complain to anyone about her, they'll take us away from her and put us in separate foster homes. We can't risk it. We need to stay together no matter what."

"What if the foster homes were all right next to each other?" Jamie asked. "Side by side. Wouldn't that be ok?"

Hannah ruffled Jamie's hair. "That's a nice thought, but it doesn't work that way. We could end up in different towns," Hannah said. "Maybe different states."

Wes was quiet until Jamie fell asleep.

"I've had enough of that old ogre, Hannah. She's meaner than dirt and getting worse. I know you always say we need to obey her rules so we don't get on her bad side, but all her sides are bad. The only thing we like about her is that she doesn't hit Jamie. There's worse things than being hit," he whispered.

"I know, Wes. I've had enough, too. I hate her. That was my last birthday gift from Mom and Dad." Hannah stared at the red mark on her wrist, her eyes starting to burn again.

"I'm sick of us not being able to play outside. We can't do anything with our school friends. We have to beg for clothes that fit. There's never enough to eat— unless your name is *Olga*. I know she's never hit Jamie, but she doesn't care that Jamie's been sick. If she cared, she would have taken him to a doctor and she would let him have one stupid hot bath. Instead, she punishes me for turning on the hot water and I'm pretty sure she would have hit him today if she could have reached him."

Jamie suddenly coughed, turned on his side and mumbled 'cops'.

"But, Wes," Hannah added, "we can't tell anybody. I don't want us to live apart from each other. Do you?"

"No. I don't know why she took us in the first place and why she doesn't want us to leave. She doesn't even like us. I think she wanted everything that used to belong to Mom and Dad. And now she's taken your bracelet. We need to do something."

"I know," Hannah agreed, then lowered her voice to a whisper. "We need to run away."

THE PLAN

Wes smiled dreamily. "Yeah, wouldn't that be cool? Wait. Do you mean it?"

"Yes. I mean it."

"Wow! First you turn on the hot water and now you're running away. Who are you and what did you do with my sister?" Wes smiled. "We should definitely run away!"

"But we can't go too far. We'll have to walk wherever we go and we'll be carrying whatever we take with us," Hannah said.

"You've been thinking about this, haven't you?" Wes asked.

Hannah nodded. "I've been dreaming about it for two years, but planning for about two hours."

"We still have the wagon Dad made for us," Wes said. "It's in the garage. We could load it up with whatever we need and head for the river. I kept one of the fishing poles and Dad's fishing tackle. We used to go bank fishing near here, remember? You can't see it from town for all the trees. We can go fishing again and we'll eat what we catch."

"I was thinking the river, too, but we don't have a tent. Could we make a shelter?"

Wes smiled. "You know my superpower is building things. We could make a shelter from pine boughs. I remember reading about that once. I'll research it more when we get to school. There are lots of caves along the river, too. A cave might make a good shelter."

"I can't wait to be outside again. At least we have a memory of it from before, but Jamie doesn't. I want him to have happy memories, too. But, what about in the winter?"

"Dad showed me how to ice fish, too," Wes said.

"But how do we keep from freezing? I don't think pine boughs will be enough protection."

"The temperature inside the caves stays in the fifties, even in winter. We just need to find a cave."

"Whoa! 50 degrees? That sounds cold."

"Hannah, what do you think the temperature is in this room in the winter? We've survived so far. We're practically polar bears."

"Remember that fireplace in the library? I always

wanted to sit there and read. We could go there to warm up," Hannah offered. "Annie told me they have free hot chocolate on Saturdays. Olga won't be able to tell us we can't go and you know she would never show up there."

"Yeah! We could go to the library." Wes' face lit up. "We wouldn't have to wait for a school field trip. We could just go."

"And I would have extra time to sketch and paint again. I would love that. Maybe I could sell some paintings to pay for food."

"Painting is your superpower. I bet you could sell them somewhere."

"I'm glad we have a plan." Hannah smiled. "It's nice to have something to look forward to for once."

And that's how Hannah's new favorite daydream was born.

They decided they would leave at the quarter break in October when they would get a day off school. Olga never paid attention to such things. They would pretend to go to school, but would circle around to the alley where their wagon of packed belongings would be waiting for them. By the time Olga realized they were late from school, they would be long gone. They couldn't trust Jamie to keep quiet about the plan, so agreed not to tell him until the morning they were leaving.

~~~

Thinking about Jamie made Hannah snap out of the daydream and back to the reality of Saturday chores. She needed to start the last load of washing, but first she would check on Jamie. Thankfully, Olga was absent—probably out for a junk food run from her favorite burger joint.

Hannah found Jamie sweeping the living room. "Hey, Jamie. I have one more load of wash to do and then I'll help you finish the floors, ok?"

"Ok, Hannah."

"If Olga comes home before then, stay out of her sight."

"Don't worry, Hannah. You know I can run faster than Ogre. 'Oh, my bunions! Oh, my bunions!'" Jamie mimed in his best Olga voice.

"Jamie, I'm being serious."

"Okay, okay. I'm sweeping. I'm sweeping."

The noise of the washing machine filling with water prevented Hannah from hearing the front door open. She finished loading the wash, closed the lid and stacked the basket in the corner. She smiled thinking about her little brother. She worried about him, true, but he was almost always happy. Jamie was definitely a vibrant orange personality. His superpower was his sense of humor. It was hard for Hannah to stay upset with Jamie because he could always make her—

SMACK! Hannah jumped, her heart racing. She held her breath hoping for silence. *Maybe Jamie dropped the broom.*

But his scream confirmed the worst.

FORGET THE PLAN

Hannah bolted down the hall and skidded into the kitchen.

Jamie ran into her arms, sobbing, clutching a greasy french-fry in his fist.

Olga set her cheeseburger on the table and wiped the grease from her chin. "Get that sniveling brat out of my sight. He can consider that stolen fry his last meal of the day."

Jamie stopped crying to look at the mangled fry he had been clutching. "Could I dip it in the ketchup?"

"Jamie," Hannah warned. "Aunt Olga, he was just hungry. He gets next to nothing for breakfast and he's too little to skip meals."

"He needs to learn manners—something your parents failed to teach you. You don't take food off another person's plate."

"If we were ever given a plate of food, then we wouldn't need to!" Hannah was afraid she may be going too far talking back to her aunt, but she was angry. She could see a large red handprint on the side of Jamie's face and it broke her heart to know that in Olga's mind, he was no longer untouchable.

Olga slammed her hand on the table. Even the plate of fries jumped. "Watch how you talk to me, girl! I deserve a medal for the sacrifices I've made to give you a home and you thank me by sassing me to defend that little thief?"

"Don't yell at my sister!" Jamie yelled. "And you're the thief. You're a bracelet stealer!" Jamie quickly scooted behind Hannah.

"Out of my sight!" Olga roared.

Without thinking about the rules, Hannah ran outside, pulling Jamie behind her. She needed to tell Wes about the latest Ogre attack, and now.

Once again, Hannah was amazed that this woman was related to them at all. *She must be one of those mutations we've been studying in science class.* It was true that the Faris children most resembled their father with their reddish-brown hair, green eyes and a sprinkling of freckles, but their mother had been a beauty and bore no resemblance to her aunt—in looks or personality.

Olga's fondness of junk food and inactivity would explain her size and maybe, somewhat, her beady eyes. But the thin lips that disappeared completely when she was angry and the dull brown hair twisted into horn-like buns did little to improve her image. Hannah was certain that Olga's heart was as dark and twisted as her hair. Hannah decided that if Olga had a color it would be puce—*like puke with a 'c'.*

"Wes!" Hannah called, waving her arms to get his attention. "Come to the alley."

Wes pushed the mower to the back of the house, then followed Hannah and Jamie.

"Uh, Hannah? What're you doing? You're not supposed to be outside," Wes said.

"Look!" Hannah pointed to the large, reddened print on Jamie's cheek.

"Oh no, Jay." Wes winced when he saw Jamie's cheek and the eyes swollen from crying. "So now she's hitting you, too? Did you try to take one of her cherry pies?" Wes had suffered a similar fate when he found his aunt's hidden stash of cherry pastries. It was then that the children realized how closely Olga kept tabs on her food, especially her favorite treats.

"No. Just one of her fries." Jamie rubbed his cheek. "She had a whole plate full. I didn't even take any of her ketchup."

"That's all it takes. Sorry she hurt you, Jamie, but you know how she is about food." Wes ruffled Jamie's hair. "How was the fry?"

"It was okay, but she said that was my last meal for the day and it didn't fill me up."

"We'll find a way to get you some food, Jamie," Hannah said. She turned away from Jamie and lowered her voice, "Wes, I don't want to wait until the quarter break. Could you be ready sooner?"

"Yeah. I've been getting my stuff ready since we first talked about it. How soon is sooner? She plays bingo tomorrow afternoon. Is that too soon?" Wes asked.

"Not for me. Tomorrow it is," Hannah said.

Jamie stepped in front of Hannah. "Talked about what? Ready for what? What happens tomorrow?" He looked at Hannah then Wes then back to Hannah. "Huh? Tell me."

"We'll tell you tomorrow afternoon, Jamie. We don't want you to spill the beans."

"What? How can I spill any beans when I can't even eat the rest of the day? Just tell me."

"No, sorry. Keep away from Olga for another day, okay? It'll be worth it. Promise. Now, come on. We need to sneak back in before Olga notices we're outside."

Later that night, after Hannah and Wes finished the dishes and scrubbed the kitchen floor, they climbed the two flights of stairs to the attic. Hannah had smuggled half of her peanut butter sandwich and a sweet pickle for Jamie. Wes saved him a glass of milk, hiding it under his shirt.

A grateful but groggy Jamie wolfed down the food and soon went to sleep.

"Poor guy has been up here alone all day. I will be so glad when we are free of that mean old bag," Hannah said.

"What do you have left to do before we leave tomorrow?" Wes whispered.

"I've been hiding some canned food and crackers behind the trunk over there, but I'm going to do one last raid on the pantry while Olga is out. She's usually gone two hours for bingo, so that will give me time to

21

finish my packing. I also washed out a couple of milk jugs that we can fill with water. It won't take long to pack our clothes. How about you?"

"I have stuff hidden in the garage—already in the wagon. I just need to gather a few more things. Jamie can help me, but not until Olga is gone. You know how he is about keeping secrets."

Jamie was lousy at keeping secrets. Olga didn't celebrate birthdays or Christmas so any gift giving was between the children and always something homemade. Last year Hannah made coloring pages for Jamie, and for Wes, she painted a catfish on one of his plain t-shirts. She made the mistake of showing the t-shirt to Jamie. He was so impressed that he immediately hunted down Wes to tell him about it— in a whisper, of course. "Hannah painted something nice on your t-shirt for Christmas, but it's a secret. Would you like it if it was a fish?"

Hannah chuckled at the memory. "You're right. That boy is terrible with secrets."

"This time tomorrow we'll be free, Hannah."

"I know. Are you a little bit scared?"

"No. We should be scared to stay here. I'm just bummed that we have to leave our school and our friends."

Hannah and Wes agreed that school would be the first place Olga would look for them. They would have to stay away.

"Me, too. Especially since we can't say goodbye to our friends and teachers. I guess I'll never know if I aced the math test," she added.

"I think we both know you did," Wes said, smiling. "So much for this year's science fair. Matt and I were going to be partners."

"Sorry, Wes. I hope we can figure out a way to go to school again."

"I know. That's ok. At least we'll be out of here."

Hannah lay awake wondering if they were doing the right thing, trying to think of everything that could go wrong and wondering if there was any other way. She glanced over at Wes. He was still awake, too.

"We'll be okay, Hannah," he whispered.

"I know. And even if we aren't, we'll be better off than we are now."

THE ESCAPE

They were careful to make sure that Sunday morning started out like all the others. Wes measured out the half cup of cereal and milk for each of them. Hannah started the coffee then prepared breakfast for Olga—two fried eggs, four strips of bacon, and two slices of toast, thick with butter and jam. Once the coffee finished, she poured a half cup, added four sugars and enough cream to fill the cup. It was tortuous for the children to smell the bacon and toast every morning, knowing they weren't allowed to have any. Even the beige coffee looked good to them.

Hannah got a sudden rebellious urge that she couldn't shake. She grabbed two strips of bacon from Olga's plate. She crumbled half of one into the waste basket and then broke the other strip in half, handing one each to her brothers. They looked at her like she had a third eye.

"Just eat them and don't say a word," she said as she popped the last piece in her mouth. She closed her eyes, chewed slowly and savored the crisp richness. She opened her eyes as she heard Olga coming down the hall toward the dining room. Wes and Jamie ate the remaining evidence, smiling at each other. Hannah grabbed Olga's breakfast plate and coffee and carried them into the dining room.

Olga's response was immediate. "Where's the rest of my bacon?" She studied Hannah so closely, Hannah was afraid she'd be able to detect bacon grease on her lips.

"They fell on the floor and broke so I threw them away. Do you want me to make more?"

"Threw them away, huh?" Olga rose from the table and went straight to the waste basket in the kitchen. She peered inside, then returned to the dining room.

"Don't let it happen again."

"I'm sure it won't, Aunt Olga." Hannah walked back to the kitchen with a big grin on her face. She gave her brothers a thumbs up and sat down to eat her cereal, wishing she could savor the taste of the sweet, crisp bacon a little longer.

The rest of the day seemed to move at a crawl, though Hannah had plenty to do. At last, the clock in the living room chimed three times. Olga stood at the door and barked out her last list of orders, which included the menu she expected for her dinner. It was to be ready at 5PM sharp.

Hannah smiled as she responded, "Yes, Aunt Olga."

Olga stopped dead in her tracks. She stared hard at Hannah, eyes beadier than usual, hair horns tilting like antenna trying to pick up a signal.

Hannah bit her lower lip. *Oops. I never should have smiled.*

"What are you up to?" Olga demanded, making her thin lips even thinner.

"N-n-nothing."

Olga stared her down, using her own form of lie detector.

Hannah dared not blink or look away.

"I don't know what you think you have to smile about, but you better not be up to something." Lips now gone. "Because if you think you've got it rough now, you just wait."

Hannah forced herself to be still until the car pulled away. "She's gone!" she called from the front door. Jamie and Wes peered into the room. "Jamie, we're running away from here—today! That's the secret. We have two hours to get everything packed and out of here so Olga doesn't see us. You help Wes load the wagon, ok?" Hannah opened the hall closet and pulled out two jugs full of water. Put these in the wagon, ok? I'm going to grab the last of the food now."

"But, wait! Won't we be in trouble?" Jamie asked. "What if Olga finds us? Where are we going, anyway?"

They answered the best they could, but that prompted more questions. "Do our teachers know? Will we be able to play outside? Can our friends come over?"

Hannah was worried about time. "We have to hurry now, Jamie, and we need you to help. We don't have all the answers but we think it's best to leave Olga now. She's getting meaner so we're going to take care of ourselves from now on, ok?"

Jamie nodded, so Hannah left him with Wes while she gathered up the remaining food.

"What do we pack for running away, Wes?"

"Think of it as camping, Jamie. Do you remember when Mom and Dad took us camping? The last time was a September day just like this one."

"Not really," Jamie said with a shrug. "I remember their faces when I look at their picture, but not much else."

Though Jamie was a toddler when they last went

camping, it was a memory Wes and Hannah held dear. Their mom would pack a cooler full of yummy food and drinks while their dad loaded the fishing and camping gear into Yellow Beauty—the name Hannah gave the family boat. It was a short drive across town to Catfish Landing where they would launch into the majestic Mississippi. Their dad guided the boat to an uninhabited sand bar. There they would pitch the tent and then fish for hours for catfish, crappie and sunfish.

While they waited for the fish to bite, they took turns using the binoculars to watch for eagles or to read the names on the tugboats going by—some of them pushing barges full of coal or grain and some of them returning on their own. They thought it was funny that the tugboats weren't 'tugging' the barges, but actually pushing them through the river. They built a campfire and roasted hot dogs and marshmallows for s'mores. When the sky grew dark enough to show off its glitter, they took turns pointing out constellations and the occasional falling star. Finally, retreating to the tent, they fell asleep to the sound of the river lapping against Yellow Beauty.

"Well, you'll like it, but we can't bring everything with us. Hannah said we could each pack one fun thing, but the rest of the wagon will be for the stuff we really need like food and water and bedding."

"What are you taking for fun, Wes?" Jamie asked.

"Dad's binoculars. I can use them to keep a lookout for any ogres."

Jamie laughed.

"We can use them to look at the moon and stars, too. Do you want to take Lion?" Wes asked.

"Yes." Jamie clutched his well-loved stuffed animal. "And my blue Blankie so Lion can sleep." Hannah and Wes knew that it was Jamie who couldn't sleep without his patch of blue blanket, now rubbed down to the size of a small hand towel. They already had it tucked inside the sleeping bag. "Can I take the glow-globe, Wes?"

Jamie loved their old globe—they all did. It was a Christmas gift to all the children and a bit of a family joke. What their parents thought was a complete globe was actually a kit with hundreds of pieces. It took their Dad two days to put it all together, but once finished and plugged in, it glowed. The light showed every mis-aligned adhesive strip, and they loved it.

Hannah entered the room in time to hear Jamie's request. "I'm sorry, Jamie. We don't have room for the globe. I wish we could take it, but we have to leave some things behind. We can't take Mom's painting easel or Wes' rock collection and basketball, either. We'll have the wagon packed tight but we need to leave room for you and Lion."

Hannah wiggled two pair of shoes she was hold-ing in her hand. "Would you guys try these on and see if they fit?" She held a pair of blue sneakers for Jamie and brown ankle boots for Wes. Sometimes, when they outgrew their shoes, she would cut the toe loose from the sole to give them a little more space and a few more weeks of wear. This delayed the unpleasant task of ask-ing their aunt for new shoes. But this time was different. Hannah didn't want them running away with shoes flip flopping.

"They fit great, Hannah, but how did you get these?" Wes asked.

She explained how she had gathered up some clothes they had outgrown and took them to the sec-ond-hand shop downtown—the Wheel and Deal Thrift Shop. She walked down last Saturday when Olga was grocery shopping.

"So, I traded for them. They are a little used, but better than what you have on now. I got these, too," she said, wiggling the toes of her pink sneakers.

"Hey, my toes don't hurt anymore. Thanks, Hannah." Jamie said. "Now I can outrun Olga for real." Jamie sprinted across the room and back to demonstrate. "What fun thing are you bringing for the run-away, Hannah?"

"I'm going to bring some of the art supplies Miss Jay gave me last year—my sketchbook and watercolors, for sure. I'm bringing your crayons, too. I'll share my paper with you."

Miss Johnson, or Miss Jay as her students called her, was Hannah's favorite teacher and not just because art was her favorite subject. Miss Jay told Hannah she was a natural. Hannah loved to hear this since her mother had been an artist. Miss Jay encouraged her to practice her sketching and painting as often as she could but there were no art supplies at home and Hannah knew better than to ask Olga for any.

On the last day of school, Miss Jay surprised Hannah with a gift of a sketchpad, pencils and a small set of watercolor paints. She had only used a handful of pages in the sketchbook, drawing at night, in the moonlight. That might explain why some of the sketches were of a very evil looking Aunt Olga. Dark room, dark subject. But there was no time to draw during the day. Hannah hoped that would change once they escaped.

"Ok, guys. I have our bedding, toothbrushes, clothing and all the food I could pack in this pillowcase. Wes, did you find Dad's canteen?"

"Yep. I've got everything on my checklist," Wes said. "I found an old grill rack in the garage, too. I cleaned it and stuck it in the wagon. Aunt Ogre won't miss it since she never used it."

"Well, she's going to miss the food and the can opener I packed, but I don't care," Hannah said, wishing she felt as brave as she sounded.

Just then they heard Olga's big boat of a Buick pull into the drive.

"Oh no! She's early. I think she knew we were up to something. Hurry. Out the back door." Hannah whispered. "I have one more thing to grab. Head down the alley like we planned. I'll catch up." Hannah ran up the stairs and grabbed a framed photo just as the car door slammed below.

Looking at the picture of her parents reminded

Hannah of one more thing. Her bracelet! Since the day Olga had taken it, Hannah had looked for it—every time she cleaned—everywhere she was *allowed* to clean. She even tried to get into Olga's desk, but it was locked. Hannah would make one more effort to locate the key. *Good thing Olga walks so slow.*

She bolted down the stairs and ran to the desk. Still locked. She glanced around the room. The key would be somewhere that is off limits to them. The bookshelf. Olga didn't have books; the shelves were full of breakable cats that they weren't allowed to touch. She started to lift the cats one by one, but stopped when she heard the front door squeak open. Hannah had a split second to get out of the room before being seen. Finding her bracelet wasn't worth the risk of spoiling all the plans they had made. She darted from the room, then tip-toed toward the back of the house.

As Hannah eased the back door open, she heard Olga muttering to herself in the kitchen, "She should be starting my dinner. I knew that girl was up to something." A cupboard door creaked open, then slammed shut.

Hannah slipped through the door, gently closing it behind her. She paused long enough to hear Olga roar, "Where in the Sam Hill are my cherry pies!"

Hannah smiled to herself as she ran to the alley.

6

SHELTER

The wagon made a terrible clattering noise as it bounced down the alley.

Aunt Olga lived in the historic part of Flinthills where the alleys were still made of brick and cobblestone. It was bumpy and hard to run on, but using the street was not an option. They didn't look like three children going to the river to fish. They looked like three children running away from home. They had to stay in the shadows as much as possible.

Wes pulled the wagon, packed so tight there was

barely room for his brother. Jamie tucked Lion under one arm as he held on tight to the sides of the wagon. Hannah jogged alongside holding a pillowcase full of clattering cans and pans.

Hannah's heart was pounding from the exertion and the fear of being caught. She continually glanced over her shoulder. If they were caught, their punishment would be worse than anything they had ever experienced before—she was sure of it! She was also sure that Jamie would be treated just as harshly as she and Wes.

"Hurry!" she called out, knowing they were already going as fast as they dared. "Turn left at the next alley by the blue house, Wes. We'll cross 5th Street and pick up the alley on the other side."

When they made the left turn, they felt a strong, cool breeze blowing in behind them. The houses along the alley had been shielding them, but now it gave them instant relief…until it began to give them concern. The wind felt good, but it came up a little too fast as the sky darkened a little too quickly. A storm was on its way.

Hannah took another look over her shoulder to make sure they weren't being followed and then stopped. "Hold up, Wes." She eased the pillowcase off her shoulder. "Nobody is following us. Let's slow down on this hill so we don't dump the wagon." She shifted her load to the other shoulder.

"Oh good 'cause my butt's sore," Jamie said.

"Here, sit on the blanket," Wes said, shoving it beneath Jamie to make him more comfortable.

By now they were several blocks from their aunt's house heading toward the downtown area. Once they reached the bottom of the hill, they turned left again. The wide, majestic Mississippi was now in view. They were only three blocks away from the bank, though about halfway to their more isolated destination.

Thunder rumbled from behind them, but not that far behind. Hannah's hair blew into her face. She took a quick look over her shoulder and knew they were in trouble. The clouds were bigger, darker and closer than they were a few minutes before. The wind blew full in her face. *This wasn't part of the plan. What else did they fail to consider?*

"Uh, Hannah?" Wes stopped the wagon. "We're about to get soaked. And we don't have anything to use as a tent."

"I know. I think we need to forget making it to the river for now. Let's find an awning on one of these buildings or something." Hannah shouted over the wind. "Wait! I know! Let's head for the Wheel and Deal Thrift

Shop. That's where I got our shoes. I remember they have a large cover over the loading dock in the back. Nobody will be there on a Sunday."

"Sounds good. Lead the way!" Wes said.

Hannah turned around, leading them away from the river. "It's just around the corner up here."

"Stop!" Jamie shouted. "Look over there, guys. That building says c-o-l-a, cola."

Hannah thought this was a poor time for Jamie to practice his spelling, but she looked across the street to where he pointed. They were looking at a large, U-shaped, three-story brick building. On one side was the faded painting of an old cola ad. There were a few broken windows and no lights on inside. The weeds in the courtyard area were as high as the rickety fence spanning the front. A 'No Trespassing' sign, mounted on the fence, flapped back and forth in the wind.

"You're right, Jamie. It does spell cola. I remember seeing this building when I went to the thrift shop last week. I'm pretty sure it's abandoned. There aren't any awnings, but maybe we can get inside," Hannah said.

"Let's check it out," Wes agreed. "That would be better than standing under an awning."

"Goody!" Jamie shouted. "Maybe they have cola in there."

They hurried across the street and stashed the wagon under a platform behind the eastern wing of the "U". Wes rushed to the corner of the building and checked the door. Locked. Hannah and Jamie followed as he tried the remaining doors. It was starting to sprinkle as they returned to the platform. Hannah was starting to lose hope.

A sudden flash of bright light lit up the sky.

Hannah gave a start. "Oh no!"

Wes started counting out loud "One Mississippi, two Mississippi..." A sudden clap of thunder made them all jump. "It's only two miles away. We need to hurry."

"Let's get under the platform!" Hannah shouted.

"What about that door?" Jamie said, pointing to a large door at the top of the platform steps. "It looks like a barn door. It has a horseshoe on it, too. See? Horseshoes bring good luck."

The three hurried up the steps, as large, cold raindrops started to pelt them. Wes tried the door, pushing in against the long metal handle. The door wiggled when pushed, but didn't open. Another bolt of lightning lit the sky, instantly followed by thunder. This time less than a Mississippi away. They were in immediate danger.

"Forget it, Wes! Let's get under the platform!" Hannah urged. But Wes continued working on the door, this time trying to slide it rather than push. Hannah saw it budge. She dropped the pillowcase of food and pulled on the door as Wes pushed. The door finally slid open wide enough for them to enter. Jamie and Wes ran inside. Hannah grabbed the pillowcase and followed.

"Oh my gosh!" Jamie said excitedly, rubbing his hands up and down his arms to dry off.

"Shhh," Wes said, with finger to lips. They all stood quietly inside, listening for any disturbance.

Jamie dropped it to a whisper, "Okay, but oh my gosh that lightning was close, you guys."

"Hello?" Wes called out to the vast, empty space. The only response was the rain pounding against the windows and partially open door.

"Anybody home?" Jamie shouted. More rain answered.

"It seems empty." Wes removed the binocular case from his shoulder and set it down with the fishing pole. "I'll get our stuff out of the wagon when the lightening moves off."

They watched out the door and listened as the

thunder moved further away. Wes made several trips to empty the wagon, handing off to Hannah inside the door. On the last trip, he shoved the wagon under the platform and ran through the door as the rain picked up velocity. Hannah helped him slide the door shut with a slam. The rusty horseshoe swung back and forth against the door.

Hannah let out a long sigh, so relieved to be out of the storm and inside a dry building. "We're safe now," she said.

Then she turned and stared into the vast and eerie darkness of her surroundings.

7

A ROOM WITH A VIEW

Wes slowly moved the flashlight all around the room.

"This is creepy," Jamie said.

Hannah stayed silent.

The dim light from the street-lamps and the sudden flashes of lightning added to the eerie feel inside. They seemed to highlight the broken glass, the cobwebs and… brooms. So many brooms.

"What's with all the brooms?" Jamie asked, picking one up and then letting it drop to the floor. "Oh no! Do you think witches live here?"

"No, Jamie. Witches don't live here," Hannah said.

"Well, is it their garage, then?" Jamie asked.

"I really don't believe in witches, Jamie, but I'm pretty sure they don't use push brooms for flight," Hannah said. "Those over there are push brooms."

"You don't know. Maybe they use those like a witch bus, or something," Jamie said.

Hannah just shook her head.

Wes shone the flashlight down the length of the first floor. "Wow. This place is huge."

"And dusty and cob-webby," Hannah said. "But at least we're out of the rain and we seem to be alone."

"There are some stairs over there," Wes said. "Let's see if the next floor looks any better. Follow right behind me in case the steps have holes."

The steps were fine, but the second floor didn't look much better than the first. If anything, it was even messier. It didn't look like any of the brooms had been used to clean the building—at least, not for many years.

"Keep going," Hannah said.

They followed Wes up to the third and final floor.

At the top of the stairs they were facing west toward a row of windows. The rain was still falling, but the clouds had parted just enough to give them a glimpse into a spectacular sunset of pinks and oranges—even more striking against the dark storm clouds.

"Ooh, look," Jamie said. "A rainbow."

"Wow," said Wes, "I haven't seen one like that before."

"It's beautiful," Hannah said. "That would make such a cool painting." She wanted to stay and imagine all the colors she would need to complete such a painting, but knew they needed to keep moving. She looked to the right and noticed a stack of wooden pallets, an old washtub, a bench and more brooms.

"Let's check out the other side, guys." Wes turned around, moving away from the stairwell. Hannah and Jamie followed. Now they were in the eastern wing where they found another row of windows just like those with the beautiful sunset. If possible, this view was even better. They were high enough to see over rooftops and chimneys clear to the river. The sunset from the west bounced off the clouds in the east and reflected off the water.

"Wait a minute. Is that the Mississippi?" Jamie asked.

"It is," Hannah said. "What a view, huh?" Hannah glanced all around her. "Look, guys, there are no broken windows and no glass on this floor. More brooms over there. You know, I bet this was an old broom factory." Hannah picked up one of the brooms and studied it more closely by the window. "This is what the label says: 'Flinthills Broomery, Flinthills, Iowa, founded in 1885. Made a mess? No need to stress!'"

43

Wes picked up another one. "This one says 'Dust in a heap? Make a clean sweep.'"

Not to be left out, Jamie grabbed one, too. "What does this one say?"

"For the cleanest room, grab a Flinthills broom!" Hannah said.

They all laughed. *Our first hour of freedom and we're laughing together—at brooms, no less.*

"I think you're right, Hannah. This must have been a broom factory. And that big platform was the loading dock. In 1885, they probably used horses and wagons to deliver the straw and wood they needed. They probably used them to deliver the brooms to stores, too."

"And one of the horses lost a shoe, so they hung it on the door so he could find it next time he came back," Jamie offered. "And it's still there waitin' for him."

"Hmmm. Maybe so," Hannah said, smiling. "Let's keep looking around."

Wes shone the flashlight down the length of the eastern wing. Hannah guessed it was at least as long as Olga's attic, probably longer. At the end, a short corridor connected it to the identical western wing. Three more windows greeted them along the side corridor.

Looking down they could see the weedy courtyard with the 'no trespassing' sign still getting tossed by the wind. A large concrete slab was directly below the windows, extending below the cola sign that first caught Jamie's eye. They had missed seeing the slab from the street because of the weeds.

"Is this a good campsite, Wes?" Jamie asked.

"I think it's pretty good, Jamie. It's not the river, but we don't want to be outside in this storm," Wes said.

"I agree," Hannah said. "Let's sleep on this top floor. I love the view of the river and we don't have any broken glass to worry about."

"You guys wait over by the stairs and I'll bring everything up to you, ok?" Wes said.

"Okay. Watch for holes in the steps," Hannah said.

It took Wes three trips to get everything upstairs. Between trips, Hannah and Jamie had each grabbed a broom and got busy sweeping an area in front of the windows with the river view. Though Jamie never got excited about cleaning anything—mostly because Aunt Olga ordered it—he was happy to help clean their new space, especially with his very own Flinthills broom.

When they finished, Hannah pried open a window. Cool, rain-freshened air gushed in. "Oh my gosh. That smells so good," Hannah said. "Come and stick your nose out here, guys."

"Fresh," Wes said.

"Mmhmm. Hannah, I'm hungry," Jamie said.

"Me too. Let's wash up and have some peanut butter and crackers. After that I have a little surprise to celebrate our first night of freedom."

"What is it, Hannah?" Jamie asked.

"Didn't I just say it was a surprise?" Hannah tweaked Jamie's nose. "You'll see."

Hannah pulled out three washcloths and three plastic cups from her backpack. Wes moistened the washcloths with water from one of the plastic jugs, then poured them each a glass of water.

"Tomorrow I'll look around for somewhere to refill our water jugs," Wes said. "If I can't find a drinking fountain downtown, I know there is one at the library. It's only a short ways up the hill."

"Yay! The library! Can I go with you, Wes?" Jamie asked.

"We'll all go, Jamie." Hannah said. "We just need

to keep watch for Aunt Ogre's Buick. If we see it, we need to hide."

"But she didn't like us. Maybe she won't bother to look for us." Jamie said.

"Maybe not, but when we don't show up at school on Monday, our teachers will wonder where we are. They might go to Olga's house to look for us. She could be in trouble if she tells them she didn't bother to try to find us or report us missing. Plus, I know she'll be mad when she sees all the food I took, and her can opener. She might come after us just to take it all back."

"Maybe we should make an ogre trap," Jamie said, giggling into his cracker.

Hannah and Wes laughed, too. *Sometimes Jamie had the best ideas.*

"When *will* we go back to school?" Jamie asked.

"Not for a while, Jamie. Olga will look for us there. Wes and I are going to be your teachers for now, okay?"

"No school?" Jamie wasn't smiling any longer.

"Are you sure we can't keep going to school, Hannah?" Wes asked. "We are only eight blocks away. We could find a way to get there that wouldn't go past

Ogre's."

"I know, but that's the first place she'll look for us. Even if we waited a week or so and then went back, we left our schoolbooks at Olga's. We would have to go back to get them before we return to school. I don't want to think about that."

"I could go get them. You and Jamie could wait in the alley for me."

"It's too risky, Wes. We've talked about this. We'll go to the library whenever we can. We can teach each other what we learn. I know we should be in school, and eventually we'll go back, but maybe to a different school. For now we just need to stay together and away from Olga."

Hannah wrapped up the crackers and put the lid on the peanut butter jar.

"What if we see some of our friends at the library?" Wes asked.

"Tell them we moved," Hannah said. "That's the truth. Just don't tell them where."

The room was suddenly quiet. It bothered Hannah that the mood had darkened with the talk of school. It also bothered her that Wes was raising questions on things they had already discussed. "Hey, if it's a nice day tomorrow, we should go fishing."

"Yeah! Fishing!" Jamie said.

"Definitely," Wes said. "If we catch any, we can build a campfire and have a fish fry, like we used to do."

Hannah was grateful to see their smiles restored. "Oh. Speaking of food, it's time for the surprise!" Hannah reached inside the pillowcase and pulled out one of Olga's forbidden pastries. "Anybody want some cherry pie?"

Jamie clapped his hands. "Really?"

Wes laughed. "Way to go, Hannah!"

They passed around the pre-packaged pie and each took a bite until it was gone. It wasn't as good as their mom's homemade pie, but it was a sweet treat they had been denied until today.

"If the ogre saw us now, she would be so mad I bet her lips and eyes would disappear like this." Jamie squinted his eyes and curled in his lips.

They all laughed, but Hannah hoped to never set eyes on the real ogre ever again.

They tired early that night and rolled out the sleeping bag on the hard, wooden floor as they had been doing in their attic bedroom night after night. They left the window open a crack so they could smell the fresh air—something they weren't able to do in their attic bedroom on any night. They snuggled under the blanket and lay still.

"Listen," Hannah whispered.

"What?" Jamie whispered back. "Did you hear a witch?"

Hannah chuckled. "No, silly. It's so peaceful." The rhythmic chirp of crickets floated up through their third-floor window. A distant train whistle and the hoot of an owl soon joined the song.

"Sweet dreams, everyone," Hannah said.

And though they weren't exactly on the river, they were very close—close enough to dream of starlit nights on a Mississippi sandbar.

~~~

But Hannah's dreams were soon interrupted. Shortly after falling asleep, she woke with a start. *Why was her heart racing? What did she just hear that made her wake up?*

She looked across the sleeping Jamie and saw Wes rubbing his eyes as he sat up.

"Did you hear that?" Hannah whispered.

"I heard something. A truck, I think. Then a loud thump."

They both pushed back the covers and hurried to the window. Headlights were moving away from behind the building. Under the streetlight they saw it was a large flat-bed truck.

Wes and Hannah looked at each other.

"Why was it here?" Hannah asked. She had a restless night thinking about the possibilities.

8

HORSESHOE HIDEOUT

A beautiful September sunrise with swirls of crimson came through the windows and shone on the sleeping children. Hannah woke first and watched Jamie stretch himself awake. *It wasn't a dream. We're free.*

"Whoa. That's bright." Jamie said, squinting and rubbing his eyes. "Hey, where are we?"

"We ran away from Aunt Ogre, remember?" Wes said, holding up his hand to shield his eyes.

"Oh yeah. I remember now." Jamie glanced down the length of the room. "We're camping at the horseshoe house."

"We are," Hannah said. "Though this is a lot bigger than any house I've ever seen." She looked around her, seeing the entire floor washed in daylight for the first time. She realized it really wasn't any worse than the first time they saw the attic bedroom they all shared at their aunt's—it was better, in fact. Here there was plenty of light and the windows opened for fresh air.

"We could almost go bowling here, it's so big," Wes said. "And there's three floors like this. It might have been Flinthills Broomery once, but it makes a good hideout now."

"Horseshoe Hideout," Jamie said.

Hannah and Wes chuckled. "That's a good name for it, Jamie," Hannah said. "It *is* a good hideout. I think we should stay here and just go to the river for fishing and exploring. It isn't very far from here."

"That sounds good to me," Wes said. "I wouldn't want to be at the river with a storm like we had yesterday."

"Good! We can start cleaning this up when we get back from the library," Hannah said.

Jamie wiggled out from under the blanket. "Uh, guys. Where's the bathroom?"

Hannah looked over Jamie's head and smiled at Wes.

"So, that's the thing about camping, Jamie," she explained. "We do most everything outside, including going to the bathroom. Let's go look for a good spot."

They put on their shoes and walked down the stairs. Hannah thought the first and second floors looked a lot less creepy in the bright sunlight, though their floor had the best view.

Wes slid the door open, looked to the left and the right, then signaled for Hannah and Jamie to follow. They walked toward the back of the building.

"So we're going to the bathroom outside like a puppy does?" Jamie asked.

"Pretty much," Hannah responded.

"Then I guess we need to find a fire hydrant!"

"We don't need to pee just like a dog, Jamie." Hannah said.

"How about behind that blue thing?" Jamie asked.

"Whoa!" Wes said, staring ahead at a bright blue plastic structure.

"Isn't that…" Hannah started to ask.

"Yes," Wes said. "It's a bathroom!"

"It is?" Jamie asked.

"It's like a portable outhouse," Wes explained. "They have them at Riverboat Days and the county fair. I wonder why it's here in the middle of nowhere." Wes looked around with a puzzled expression on his face.

"Wes," Hannah said. "Do you think this is what we heard go thump last night?"

"Oh, yeah. I bet it was. The truck came from this direction, didn't it?"

Strange though it was, it was also very convenient.

Once they were back inside, they washed their hands, brushed their teeth and ate a quick breakfast. By now, one of the plastic water jugs was nearly empty.

"Let's roll up the bedding and put away the food before we go to the library," Hannah said. She removed her art supplies and clothing from her backpack and put the empty canteen and water jug inside. It was time for a field trip to explore their new neighborhood and to fetch water. Jamie grabbed Lion and off they went.

Wes slid the door open, peaked outside, then signaled for Hannah and Jamie to follow. They walked down the steps and turned toward the street.

"I think we should stick with the alleys just in case and then…HIDE!" Wes shouted. He slammed his back flat against the brick building and held his arm out to stop Jamie. Looking sideways toward the street, they saw a big brown Buick driving in their direction, way below the speed limit. Aunt Ogre! She was looking to her left, across the street from their building, but as soon as she turned her head to the right she would see them.

"Drop down!" Wes whispered as he pulled Jamie

to the ground.

Hannah followed. They crouched in the weeds as best they could. Hannah watched as the Buick continued slowly past them. She let out her breath and started to rise when suddenly the lights at the back of Olga's car lit up. Olga was stopped in the middle of the street, just twenty some feet in front of them. Hannah crouched lower into the weeds.

"Why did she stop? What did she see?" Wes whispered, certain that the three of them were well hidden. He looked to his right, following Aunt Ogre's line of vision. "Oh no."

Hannah looked toward the platform. Their one-of-a-kind wagon was under the platform, but not completely hidden. Her heart started to pound in her chest. If Olga got out of her car, they needed to run.

Jamie suddenly started wiggling in the weeds. "This grass is tickling my no-ha-HA-CHOO!"

Oh no! Hannah thought. The three of them froze.

The car door opened. Horn buns slowly rose up from the car and then the rest of her. Olga stood in the street and stared where they were crouched.

We should run! Hannah thought. She reached for Jamie but waited for the right moment.

Suddenly, Olga darted her head from side to side. She spun around and raised her arms, swinging them wildly around her head. Finally, she smacked herself hard on the side of her face.

Wes snorted.

Jamie covered his mouth to stifle his giggles.

"Shhhh," Hannah warned.

A bug. *A perfectly placed, biting bug!* Without giving them another glance, Olga dove into her car, slammed the door and rolled up the windows. She drove to the end of the block and made a slow right turn.

"She's going to circle around and come back to look again. I'm hiding the wagon before she comes back," Wes said. "Maybe she'll move on if she doesn't see it again."

Wes moved the wagon to the opposite side of the loading dock so it couldn't be seen from the street. They all dashed across the street and into the opposite alley. They hid behind a utility box until the Buick came by again.

"Well, now we know. She's definitely looking for us," Hannah said.

Olga didn't stop this time and didn't even glance

to her left where they were hiding. Her eyes were glued to the platform where she likely had seen the wagon. Once she was out of sight, the children continued up the alley—the alley between the art center and the antique store.

"Hey, a faucet," Hannah said, pointing at the wall outside the art center. "They must have it there for clean-up when they have outdoor classes. I wonder if it works."

Wes crouched down and turned the knob. He jumped backwards to avoid the gush of water. "It works, alright."

"This will be perfect to fill our bucket for cleaning," Hannah said. "We probably still want to use the library water for drinking whenever we can, though. It comes from a cooler."

"For cleaning what?" Jamie asked.

"The dishes, our clothes, ourselves," Hannah said.

"Oh no. More cold baths?"

"And in a bucket," Wes said, rolling his eyes.

"Well, not a bath, exactly," Hannah said. "But we don't want to turn into slobs." She had packed washcloths, towels and soap, but that's as far as she got with her planning. They knew better than to consider river water for getting clean. Even if they found a slough that would keep them out of the dangerous current, it was called the Muddy Mississippi for good reason.

They crossed the main street downtown. Not a brown car in sight. Hannah was a little uncomfortable walking back uphill toward Aunt Ogre's house, but she knew they would never see *her* at the library. She thought reading was a waste of time and couldn't be bothered to get them a library card. Hannah's third grade teacher, Miss Orr, took the class on a field trip to the library and helped Hannah get her own card. She treasured it and kept it with her always.

The library was rarely busy on a Monday morning. That was good, and that was bad. They weren't likely to see any of their school friends here (good), but the librarians might wonder why they weren't in school (bad). Wes took the canteen and water jug out of the backpack and filled them at the water cooler near the restrooms. Fortunately, nobody seemed to notice them.

"Can we get some books while we're here, Hannah?" Jamie asked.

"I'd like to, but the librarians might wonder why we aren't in school."

"We'll just tell them we're running late, but that we really, really needed some books. They love it when you say things like that," Wes said.

"Yeah, we'll tell them we're having a book emergency," Jamie added.

"Ok. I'll help you pick out some books, Jamie, then you can help me find one for myself. Wes, why don't you get one, too, and then meet us back in the picture book section when you're done."

"Sounds good. I'm going to get on the computer for a few minutes first."

Jamie picked out several picture books that featured an animal of some sort. He loved lions, of course, but loved pictures of any four-legged creature. Hannah selected an easy reader and an ABC book for him, too. She picked out a Nancy Drew mystery for herself. She was halfway through the series and determined to read every one. Her mother had read them all when she was little, and that's how Hannah got hooked on them. The original series was a little old-fashioned, but the mysteries were fun to try to solve.

Wes spent most of his time on the computer, but then found a book and returned to the picture book section.

"What did you find on the computer, Wes?" Jamie asked.

"Oh, just some fun facts about the Mississippi."

"Ooh. Cool picture of an axe," Jamie said, pointing to Wes' book selection.

"It's a hatchet. See this word. H-A-T-C-H-E-T. Hatchet."

"Oh, I heard that was a good book," Hannah said.

"You can read it when I'm done."

"Thanks. You can read my Nancy Drew book when I'm done, too."

"Uh. No thanks."

Hannah knew what he was thinking. "It's not just for girls, Wes. It's mystery and adventure."

"For girls."

Hannah rolled her eyes. "Whatever."

The librarian was all smiles when they checked out their books. "It looks like you made some wonderful selections!" she said.

"I hope so," Jamie said, smiling back. "We're

going to teach each other..."

Hannah quickly interrupted as she reached for the books. "Thank you very much! Let's go guys." She shoved the books into the backpack and rushed them out the door.

"Jamie!" Hannah started, once they were outside.

"Shush, Hannah," Jamie said. "Everything is fine. I want to hear a Mississippi fun fact, Wes."

"Ok, but you need to remember to keep our secrets to yourself, Jay," Wes said.

"Ok, ok."

"So!" Wes began. "I found out the Mississippi River begins at a small lake in Minnesota—Lake Itasca. It takes water three whole months to go from Lake Itasca all the way down to Pilottown, Louisiana."

"Wow. That sounds like a long time," Jamie said. "How many days are in three months?"

"It's about 90 days."

"But where's Minnesota and where's the pilot's town?"

"Next time we go to the library, I'll show you.

Minnesota is a state like Iowa and it's right above us on the map so north of us. Lake Itasca is in the northern part of Minnesota, pretty close to Canada, really. Pilottown is a town just like Flinthills is a town. It's just south of New Orleans in the state of Louisiana. That's where the river finally dumps into the Gulf of Mexico," Wes said.

"Oh, I remember the Gulf of Mexico from our globe," Jamie said.

"That just doesn't seem right," Hannah said. "So if I dropped a feather in Lake Itasca, it would take three months for the feather to dump into the gulf? It seems like it's going a lot faster than that."

"I know. I thought the same thing. It said most grown-ups can walk faster than the river flows."

"We should try it someday!" Jamie said.

"Someday," Wes said. "You're not a grown up yet, you know."

Once they had returned to Horseshoe Hideout, they all chipped in to get it cleaned and organized. They were used to working together and did it well. Unlike some brothers and sisters, they rarely fought with each other—probably because they were united against a common enemy. They were more into survival mode than most kids their age, so had better things to do than pick fights with each other.

"I'll go to the alley and fill our bucket at that faucet we found," Wes said.

"Thanks, Wes. Watch out for the ogre," Hannah said.

While Wes was fetching water, Jamie helped Hannah move some found items into their space. The wash tub would be useful. They found a sturdy table and a bench that would be perfect for their meals and for storing their dishes. They put their rolled-up sleeping bag and blanket on the bench while they swept the area.

Wes returned with a bucket of water that he dumped into the wash tub. "You can use that to wash the floors and I'll go get another for the table and bench."

Hannah tied a towel around the broom and used it as a wet mop to clean the floor. When the washtub appeared to be holding more mud than water, she stopped and decided it was good enough for the time being.

Wes cleaned the table and bench, then washed their row of windows as far as he could reach. He pushed one open to let in fresh air to help dry the floor. Wes bailed the muddy water back into the bucket and hauled it downstairs to empty. Hannah worked on sweeping down cobwebs. She found a couple hooks on the walls she used to hang up their extra clothing, towels, binoculars and backpack.

"Too bad we don't have more hooks," she said, when Wes returned.

Wes looked at the overloaded hooks. "I have an idea. Let me see if there are any nails in the toolbox I brought." He opened the little red toolbox that used to belong to their dad and pulled out a hammer. "Oh good. These will work."

"Oh, yeah. We can use nails for hooks, huh?" Hannah asked.

"We could. But I want to try something else," Wes said. He picked out two of the shorter brooms with skinnier handles. He placed them about shoulder height off the floor, horizontally, across two of the upright beams. "Hold this here, Hannah."

While Hannah held the broom in place, Wes nailed one end down. He stood back to look at his work. "Raise it a little bit on that side, Hannah. There!" Then he nailed the other end.

He repeated the same process with the second

broom. When he was done, they had a length of rod for hanging clothes and towels and anything else they could drape.

"Instant closet. Nice, Wes!" Hannah said.

"Thanks. I need to get one more bucket of water."

Jamie helped Hannah set their candles, canteen and dishes on the table and pushed the bench underneath for seating. They put their rolled-up sleeping bag and blanket against the wall opposite the table. They found an old crate, swept it off, and turned it on end to use as a small table to hold their library books, art supplies and the framed photo of their parents that Hannah had rescued from Aunt Olga's. Lion and Blankie sat perched on top of the sleeping bag where Jamie could keep an eye on both.

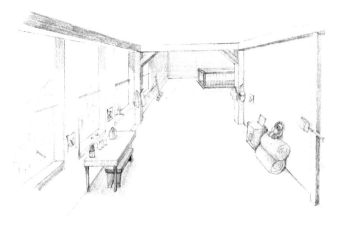

"Wow. This is looking nice," Wes said, when he returned. "Here, I brought some fresh water so we can wash up without getting into our drinking water."

"Ah, good. Let's have lunch at our new table," Hannah said. "We'll have a peanut butter and jelly sandwich with pork and beans. Jamie, you can get three plates and forks, okay?"

Wes poured them each a cup of water and they all sat down to enjoy a well-deserved meal. "Save the bean can. We'll rinse it out and use it to dig for worms."

"I wanna help dig," Jamie said.

"Oh, don't worry. You'll be our official—" But Wes didn't get a chance to finish what he was going to say.

A loud slam came from outside the open window. They all got up from the bench to look out. Another loud slam soon followed, then another.

Several men were outside unloading bundles from a truck and plopping them onto their platform.

"Back away from the window," Hannah whispered, fearful the workmen would look up and see them.

"They're shingles," Wes said.

"Oh great," Hannah said.

"Oh great," Jamie echoed. "But what are shingles?"

Just then the sliding door opened on the first floor. They heard muffled voices.

"Shhh," Hannah gestured.

Jamie slapped his hand over his mouth, eyes nearly popping out of his head.

Frozen in place with their backs flat against the wall, they watched the stairwell, fearful they were about to be found out. But nobody came up. Finally, the door slid shut and the voices ceased. They glanced out the window and watched the vehicles leave the premises.

Hannah sagged back onto the bench.

"Shingles go on the roof, Jamie," Wes explained. "They are going to put new shingles on our roof which means there will be a bunch of men working here."

"That's why there is a portable bathroom in back yard and that's why we shouldn't get too comfortable," Hannah warned.

9

THE MISSISSIPPI

The workmen didn't return that day. It was time to go fishing.

"Come on, Jamie. Help me dig for worms. They come out of the ground when it rains so we won't have to dig very deep," Wes said.

He was right. Before long they had a can full of fat night-crawlers. They packed the wagon with tackle box, cooking supplies, water and matches. Wes carried his Zebco 33 CustomZ fishing pole—'old blue', as his Dad called it—and they headed for the river. They needed to go about five blocks, but they took side streets and alleys to ensure they would go unnoticed, keeping an eye out for Olga the whole time.

"Do you remember how to get to our spot, Wes?" Hannah asked. "Weren't there some funny trees we used as landmarks?"

"Yes, there were three, remember? The one at the trailhead had an owl face where those twin branches had fallen and left hollowed out eyes. We turn left there and walk until we see the tree with the big nose and one eye. We turn right and walk until we reach the tree that looks like it has a big open mouth. Dad told us to watch for the eyes, the nose and the mouth and we'll be there"

"I hope the trees are still there," Hannah said.

"I wanna see if I can pick them out," Jamie said.

Before long they left the pavement of the town and entered the wooded area leading to the river.

"I see the owl tree over there!" Jamie said, laughing. "It has to be the one."

"It is!" Hannah said, relieved to see the old landmark looking just as owl-like as before. *It was almost like having Dad along to guide them.*

"Ok, go this way now," Wes directed.

"Look at the big nose and the one eye!" Jamie was jumping from the excitement of his discoveries. "I'm just as good as Nancy Drew, huh, Hannah? What's my next clue?"

"This way," Wes said, turning right at the nose tree. "You need to find a big open mouth."

"A big open mouth. A big open mouth. A big open...I see it! I see it!" Jamie ran ahead to the tree with the wide-open mouth. "It even has a tongue sticking out of its mouth."

"That's it! Here's the spot alright," Hannah said, taking a moment to look around. They were in a small clearing with a patch of sandy beach protected from the strong current of the main channel, tucked between pine and oak trees. It was private, shady and had a large fallen tree limb for seating. Just as it was two years before.

"It's still so beautiful. Just how I remember it," Hannah said. *So many happy times here, and yet she wanted to cry.* Her parents were gone and her kind teachers and best friend were no longer a part of her life. Hannah suddenly realized how much she wanted a caring adult in her life. She wanted to be a child again, especially here. She looked up to find Wes staring at her. *I wonder if he feels it, too.*

"Uh, guys. Is this a staring contest or something? Shouldn't we fish?" Jamie asked.

Thank goodness for Jamie and thank goodness he's always so happy. Hannah blinked back the threatening tears, determined to make a happy memory. "Yes, we should. Let's have Wes fish first while you help me find some firewood, okay? We'll look under that big evergreen tree over there. You take the bucket and pick up little sticks and dried pine needles that we can use for kindling."

"I'm on it! Catch a big one, Wes 'cause I'm hungry." Jamie said.

"I'll try. Hey, I put pieces of a broken broom and handle in the wagon in case you don't find any dry wood," Wes said. He dug in the can for a fat night-crawler and baited the hook.

Remembering what their dad taught him, he placed his thumb on the release while firmly grasping the reel in his hand. He made a wide sideways motion with his arm as he released his thumb. He watched the hook and nightcrawler fly gracefully through the air, over the water, leading a long length of line with it. The weighted line finally dropped into the water and sank several feet as the current pulled it downstream.

Wes gave the crank on the reel a short turn until he heard the click. The line was set. He sat down on the huge fallen log without taking his eye off the water.

"Don't get too relaxed over there," Hannah teased. "Are you holding your thumb against the line like Dad taught us?"

"Yep. I remember."

"And watch the end of your pole to see if it moves."

"And if I get a bite, I'll jerk the line backwards to set the hook. I know."

Luckily, the wood under the ever-green trees felt dry. Jamie filled the bucket with kindling while Hannah picked up the bigger sticks.

"Now let's look for some boulders to line our fire pit, Jamie. Something about this size or a little bigger." Hannah held up a small boulder in her fist.

"You mean like those over there?" Jamie pointed to what was obviously somebody's old fire pit.

"Oh, wow. That's perfect, Jamie. That might be the one we used to use. Let's build our fire there." Hannah gathered a fist full of the dried pine needles and leaves from the bucket. She formed them into a small, loose nest. She took the smallest of the sticks and formed a small tepee around the nest.

"Are you just playing, Hannah?" Jamie asked.

"No. First you make a small nest with the smallest bits of leaves or straw. It needs to be nice and airy because fire needs air to burn. That's where we'll put the lit match. It's the easiest thing to catch fire quickly. Then it will catch these little sticks on fire that we are putting around the nest. We'll keep doing this, using larger sticks with each tepee. If we do it right and the wood is dry, we'll have a nice strong fire."

Hannah struck a match and gently placed it inside

the small nest she had made. It instantly lit the kindling and continued to grow.

"Look, Wes," Jamie said. "We're burning all the tepees."

"Good job, bud. Now let's see if I can catch something to put on the fire."

Hannah brought a can of pork and beans to cook over the fire, too. Even if they failed to catch a fish, they would have something to eat.

Tonight that wouldn't be a problem. Suddenly, Wes jumped to his feet and yanked the pole backwards. He started to reel in the line, bending forward as he reeled and then pulling back on the pole.

"Oh my gosh! It must be a big one." Hannah said. "Look how the pole is bending."

"It's a whale!" Jamie shouted, clapping his hands.

"I might need help," Wes groaned, reeling in with everything he had.

"What do you want me to do?" Hannah asked. "I wish we had a net! Do you want me to take a turn reeling it in?"

But with one last heave, Wes landed the fish – the

biggest catfish he had ever caught. He set down the pole and shook his arms. "Man, that was heavy. I'm glad it didn't break old blue. This is going to take me awhile to clean. Who wants to go next?"

"I do!" Jamie said.

Wes looked at Hannah.

She nodded. "Let Jamie go. I want to keep an eye on the fire. But you need to sit on the log, Jamie. Okay?"

"I will," Jamie said.

Wes removed his catch and secured it on a nearby boulder. He re-baited the hook, cast it into the water for Jamie, and then started to clean his catch.

Hannah was impressed that Wes remembered how to clean the fish. She loved to fish but wasn't big on the cleaning part. She put the skillet on the fire to heat up.

Suddenly, Jamie jumped up from the log and let out a yelp. "I have one! I have one!"

"Yank back on the pole quick and hard to set the hook, Jamie," Wes instructed as he ran to his brother's side to help.

Jamie had already started frantically reeling in the line, so when he finally yanked backwards as Wes instructed, the line was too short. The small sunfish went sailing into the air behind him.

"Catch him, Wes!" Jamie shouted as he watched his first catch free fall into the kindling bucket.

The three were laughing hysterically as they looked into the bucket.

"This little guy was caught twice," Wes said. "Once on your line and once in the bucket. It's a sunfish, Jamie. This kind is called a blue gill. See this little blue flap on the gill? That's how you know."

Jamie beamed from ear to ear and sighed. "I caught a flying sunfish."

"I think we have enough to eat, though, and this little guy worked pretty hard to get free. Shall we let him go?" Wes asked.

"Sure, but I wanna throw him back in." Jamie handled him as Wes instructed, with thumb wedged under his gill and finger inside the mouth. He walked carefully to the riverbank, giggling. "He's tickling my thumb!" He flung the fish back into the river and watched him swim away. "Bye, Sunny. There he goes, heading to New Orleans."

They soon sat down to a plate of delicious fish

and beans.

"This is the best day ever," Jamie said.

"And this is our best meal ever," Wes said.

"It's almost perfect, isn't it?" Hannah asked. "Even more perfect if we had a baked potato to go with it."

"And some coleslaw," Wes said.

"And some ice cream and chocolate cake," Jamie said.

Hannah laughed. "Do you even remember ice cream and chocolate cake, Jamie?"

"No, but that's what everyone at school wants on their birthday, so it must be good."

They didn't have a refrigerator to store fish, and it was starting to get dark, so they decided not to do anymore fishing that night. They set the remaining night-crawlers free, removed the grill from the fire to cool it down and rubbed sand in the skillet to clean it out. While they waited for the fire to burn out, they watched the sunset bounce off the cottony clouds slowly drifting by. They loaded up the wagon to the sounds of crickets chirping, bull frogs croaking and water lapping gently against the shore.

Walking back, Wes interrupted the silence. "Hey. You know when we were at the library and I was researching on the computer?"

"Yeah, about the Mississippi, right?" Jamie asked.

"Yeah, but I was also checking to see if there was anything about horseshoe's bringing good luck."

Jamie looked up at Wes, eagerly waiting for the news. "I was right, wasn't I?" he asked.

"Well, that's what some people think—for hundreds of years, actually. But they can't agree on how you should hang the horseshoe to bring the good luck. Sailors say you should hang the horseshoe so the open end is up. That way it'll catch all the good luck. But fisherman say the open end should be down so the good luck goes into their nets and they catch a lot of fish."

"See!" Jamie said, excitedly. "Ours is pointing down and we caught two fish!"

Hannah smiled to herself, but as soon as the trees started to thin, her smile was gone. Once on the pavement, she looked from side to side, every headlight a reason for concern. They needed to watch for Olga's car again. And there would be shingles stacked on the loading dock at their hideout. *They were going to need a lot of luck from that horseshoe.*

10

WEEK ONE

It had been a week since the workmen dropped off the stack of shingles, and they hadn't returned. The children hadn't seen Aunt Olga again, either. Though constantly on the look-out, they were comfortable in their hideout and into a daily routine.

Water fetching was a must. They all went to the library for the drinking water, but primarily when they weren't expected to be in school. When Wes went to the alley for cleaning water, Hannah kept look-out. She pushed the window open so Wes could hear her warning signal, if needed.

Jamie was helping her watch. "What's the signal, Hannah?"

"I'll whistle like a bob-white, just like Dad used to do when we were at the park or the store and it was time to go."

"I don't remember that. What's a bob-white?" Jamie asked.

"It's a bird, another name for a quail. They whistle like this…" Hannah stepped away from the window and demonstrated with a low whistle followed by a high whistle, then two identical low whistles followed by a high whistle.

"Like this? Bob-white! Bob-bob-white!" Jamie didn't know how to whistle, so sang the signal.

Hannah laughed. "Well, you've got the melody, anyway. One of these days I'll teach you to whistle."

So far, they had never had to use their warning system, which was fine with Hannah. She wasn't sure what Wes should do if someone was on the premises, but it felt good to have half of a plan, anyway.

Besides fetching water, searching for workmen and eating three small meals each day, they always did some form of schoolwork. They took turns helping Jamie with his reading, counting and forming his letters. They also shared fun facts, Wes' specialty.

"It's fun fact Monday, everyone. Who wants to go first?"

"I do," Jamie said. "What does this spell, everybody: M-I-S-S-I-S-S-I-P-P-I?"

"Mississippi," Wes and Hannah answered together.

"That's right," Jamie said. "It's fun to say, isn't it?

Especially I-P-P." Jamie laughed.

"Ok, Jamie." Hannah rolled her eyes.

"Well, speaking of the Mississippi, here's another fun fact," Wes said. "Did you know that here in Flinthills the river is usually less than 20 feet deep, but in New Orleans it can be 200 feet deep?"

Jamie's eyes were like silver dollars. "Is that taller than this building, Wes?"

"Yes, way taller."

"Whoa. We would drownded in New Orleans."

"We would *drown*, you mean," Hannah said.

"No. I mean we would drown *dead*, Hannah," Jamie corrected.

Hannah grinned. "Ok. So let's just agree that we won't be swimming in the Mississippi—here or in New Orleans—without a life jacket and then we won't need to worry about drowning or drowning dead, okay?"

When Wes took a turn helping Jamie with his schoolwork, Hannah would draw or paint. She had shared some of her sketchbook paper with Jamie and Wes, so the remaining pages were filling up fast. She had sketches of their hideout, the river and the three special landmark trees. She also drew pictures of the birds and butterflies she saw when she was outside. Her drawings were definitely cheerier than the ones she sketched in the attic.

One day while she and Wes were hanging up their washed clothing on the broomstick rods, Jamie asked if he could use a page from her sketchbook.

"Sure, but can you get it? My hands are all wet. Just make sure you're pulling out a blank page and be gentle when you pull it out."

Minutes later she glanced over to make sure Jamie didn't need help. He was studying a drawing in the sketchbook that Hannah had made when they were still at Olga's. Hannah had torn it out planning to throw it away, but she hadn't. It was a drawing of evil-eyed Olga that she had sketched in haste after the hot water incident.

"Oh, wait, Jamie. I'll get you one," Hannah said, wiping her hands on the side of her jeans.

"This is scary, Hannah," Jamie said.

"Sorry. I didn't mean for you to see that. I was just doodling. Here you go! A nice fresh sheet. Use up all the space on it because we're running low, okay?" Hannah stuck the drawing back inside the cover. She would have to remember to use it as kindling for their next fire.

Though going to the river was their favorite group activity, the weather didn't always cooperate. On those days they entertained themselves indoors. The hideout had many rooms to explore. It was perfect for a game of hide-and-go-seek.

They also made up games, many of them involving brooms: held backwards, the brooms made good hockey sticks; the smaller brooms worked well for sword fights; the push brooms were used for racing or for giving Jamie rides; and what hideout with the first name of horseshoe would be complete without a horse? Jamie had a favorite broom he named Dust Devil. Before long, their sweeping games had cleared most of the debris on all three floors.

"I can make us a checkerboard on my sketch paper," Hannah said. "You guys can search through the rocks we've collected from the river and separate them by color. The limestone rocks are all white so that can be one set. You can use the smooth river rocks for the other set. Just pick small ones so they'll fit on a board this small." Hannah held up a sheet of sketch paper.

"Jamie, you can pick out the white ones. We need twelve," Wes said.

With the board complete and the rocks all selected, they played checkers, endlessly. Jamie couldn't get enough, but it didn't take long for Wes and Hannah to get a little bored.

"Chess is way more fun," Wes said.

"Oh, I love chess," Hannah agreed. "But I don't remember all the moves."

"I do. We played at school whenever we had indoor recess. Let's make some chess pieces," Wes suggested. "We can play when Jamie is busy with his reading or when he conks out."

"Ok. We can use the checkers as the pawns and make the fancier pieces."

Wes used his fishing knife and sticks they found on the property to whittle wooden bases for the paper faces Hannah painted—pale gray for the limestone set of pawns and brown to match the river rock pawns. On nights that Jamie conked out early, they lit candles and set up the chess board for a game.

"Now we just need a bowl of popcorn," Hannah said.

"Or chocolate cake and ice cream," Wes said, smiling.

Hannah giggled. "Shhhh. You'll have Jamie

dreaming about it."

They didn't have many things, so threw away nothing and found a use for everything they kept. Wes used their empty cans to make an ogre trap. He stacked them up by the door and showed Hannah and Jamie what would happen if Olga or anyone else came in and stumbled over them.

"But, Wes. The workmen came inside once," Hannah said. "If they knock over a stack of cans by the door the next time they come in, they'll know someone is inside and they'll come looking for us."

"Oh, duh. You're right."

"But they would make great bowling pins," Hannah said.

So, they scrapped the idea of the ogre trap and stacked the cans at the end of their long empty hall for bowling. They used a pair of rolled up socks as the bowling ball, easier thrown than rolled.

But one of their favorite indoor activities was 'watching TV', as Wes called it.

"Hey, you guys want to watch TV?" he asked one evening, as he gazed outside through the binoculars.

"Wes, don't tease," Hannah said. Aunt Ogre had a TV, but the only time the children could watch was if she fell asleep with it on. Once they heard her loud snores drift up the stairs, they would sneak down to see if she was watching anything they might want to watch. They didn't dare change the channel and couldn't turn up the volume to hear over Olga's snoring, so it wasn't a great experience. Their friends at school talked about their favorite TV shows, but Hannah, Wes and Jamie couldn't really relate.

"I'm not teasing. This is what's showing right now," Wes said. "It's the Mr. Crane show. Mr. Crane just finished his dinner of salmon patties, peas and tea. Now he's decided to sit on his porch to enjoy a bit of fresh air before it gets dark. But his lawn chair is wet from the rain, so he has to dry it off first. Now he is taking off his shoes and his socks and he's–ew—clipping his toenails."

Jamie laughed. "How do you know his name is Mr. Crane?"

"Because. He's tall and thin and leans forward like a crane and has a long nose like a beak. He just has to be a Mr. Crane."

"And how do you know what he had for dinner?"

Hannah asked.

"It's my TV show. I can decide."

"I wanna see." Jamie pulled the bench to the window for a better view. Wes handed him the binoculars, pointing them in the vicinity of Mr. Crane. "Yep, there he is. He's all done and putting his shoes and socks back on. He went in the house. Wait, what's the smoke? Oh! The man and lady in the yard next to him are having a cook-out. Let's open the window to see if we can smell it!"

"Let me see," Wes said. He opened the window a crack and took the binoculars back. "They're on the other side of the fence from Mr. Crane. They must have kids. There's a little plastic pool set up on the patio. I only see a man and woman outside, though."

Jamie stuck his nose out the window. "Mmmm," was all he said.

"My turn to look," Hannah said, reaching for the binoculars. "Ah. I think I smell hot dogs. The woman is putting her feet in the pool. Maybe it's hers. Maybe she works on her feet all day, or maybe she wears those pointy-toed high heel shoes like Miss Orr. Wow. They have a pretty garden."

"You and your flowers, Hannah," Jamie said,

rolling his eyes.

"The flowers are pretty, but they have a huge vegetable garden, too." Hannah handed the binoculars to Jamie.

"I want to sit in the pool and eat a hot dog," Jamie said. "And then have some chocolate cake and ice cream."

They all laughed.

But the talk of hot dogs and other food was a harsh reminder of their own reality. They were running dangerously low on food.

11

WILL PAINT FOR FOOD

Hannah reviewed the food supply the next morning. They had one can of pork and beans left and one sleeve of crackers. There was enough peanut butter and bread for each to have another sandwich—a half sandwich, really. They would go fishing whenever they could, but not three times a day and there were no guarantees they would catch something.

Hannah had to do something about it. She picked out a few of the drawings that she thought were her best. She poured a little water into an empty bean can and used it to add touches of watercolor—a little Caribbean blue on the butterfly, a splash of cadmium yellow on the flower and a little sap green for the river scene. Once dry, she pressed them under the library books to get out the wrinkles. Real artists signed their names on their paintings, but Hannah didn't want strangers to know her name so she used her initials—hlf—Hannah Lynn Faris. *There. Almost a real artist.*

Hannah took a deep breath. "I am going to the art center to see if I can sell these," she said.

"Do you want us to come with you?" Wes asked.

"No. Why don't you and Jamie start working on

the courtyard, like we talked about. I'll try not to take too long."

Wes and Hannah had talked about trying to clean up some of the weeds in the courtyard area—behind the fence with the No Trespassing sign. One day, while playing hide-and-go-seek, they had found a door on the first floor that opened into the courtyard—right onto the big cement slab. With the weeds gone, they might be able to have an outdoor play area and maybe a fire pit.

"Ok, we'll get started on it," Wes said. "Good luck!"

"Hannah, see if you can buy some hot dogs," Jamie said.

Hannah wasn't feeling especially confident with her ability to sell her paintings, but she knew she had to try. "I can't promise anything, Jamie." She grabbed the empty backpack and her paintings. "Here goes!"

Hannah lingered outside the art center until the few customers inside had all left. When she entered, she was greeted with the sound of a tinkling bell that was attached to the door. The walls inside were covered with an assortment of framed paintings, shelves of glazed pottery and a turn-style stand of homemade jewelry. Hannah was in awe, but also disappointed that her own work seemed so small and not quite worthy.

"May I help you?" asked the young woman behind the counter.

"Oh, well, I was wondering if…I mean, how do people sell their art here?"

"Well, they fill out a request form and present us with a sample of their art —a picture of it is fine—and at the next board meeting, the members vote to see if they will allow the art to be sold. If so, then the artist sets a price and fills out a form with the description and other details. We allow each piece to be on display for three months and if it doesn't sell, then we ask the artist to bring in something new."

"If it doesn't sell?" Hannah looked shocked. "It can take three months?"

"Sadly, most pieces don't sell, but some artists do well. I should add, you need to be 18 or older to sell in the gallery, though we do have a semi-annual show for student artists. Let's see. Yes, the next one will be December first. Are you interested in participating?"

Hannah's shoulders sagged. "I didn't know it worked that way. I didn't know it would take so long. I…but thank you."

As Hannah turned for the door, a painting caught her eye. It must have been the brilliant colors the artist used, because the subject was just a basket of vegetables. Nothing very exciting, but Hannah stared at it for some time while an idea began to form.

"Aren't those lovely colors?" the clerk asked.

"Delicious!" Hannah said.

She practically ran down the alley, stopping to look for traffic before she crossed near Horseshoe Hideout and continued on until she was in front of the house with the large garden. She knew it was the right house because the small blue pool was sitting by the curb. There was no car in the driveway and nobody in the front yard. She hurried down the side yard along the fence that separated the garden house from Mr. Crane's, her heart almost pounding out of her chest.

The yard was even lovelier in person. Hannah wanted to take her time to smell the flowers, sit under the shade of the trees and smell the clothes that were hanging on the line. It felt like a real home. But she knew she couldn't risk getting caught, so hurried.

She took two paintings from the backpack, hurriedly wrote 'Thank you for the vegetables!' on the back of one and clipped them both to the clothesline. Then she ran to the vegetable bed. She loved how the bean plants looked like a mass of leaves until you really studied them and realized they were covered in a gazillion beans. The cucumber vine was even more secretive with its fruit. It appeared to be a long vine of bright green leaves trailing on the ground—but Hannah lifted a leaf and discovered big and juicy cucumbers.

There was no hiding the bright red tomatoes bursting out of their wire cages. She popped a bean into her mouth as she picked a few onions and puzzled over the dark green plants in front of her. *Oh yeah! Potatoes!* She remembered from gardening with her mother that she shouldn't try to pull on the plants to unearth the potatoes. She would need a shovel or pitchfork to dig them up.

She glanced around the yard and spotted a small shovel propped against a quaint garden shed. She used it to turn over one of the plants and was rewarded with several small red potatoes. She new that the feathery plants at the end of garden were carrots, so pulled up a few of those. The backpack was feeling heavy now and she didn't want to take more than her paintings were worth, so decided to put the shovel away and leave.

In her haste, Hannah didn't get the shovel safely propped against the shed. She grabbed for it but not before it had crashed against the door and onto the concrete slab with a clang. She quickly looked around the yard to see if she had been found out. That's when she spotted an indigo colored butterfly flitting around a large shrub by the clothesline. She walked toward it for a better look and realized the shrub was covered with blackberries. Hannah opened the backpack once more and gently dropped some berries inside.

As she left the yard, she studied the wading pool by the street. It was made of a stiff plastic, but had a crack on one side of the rim. It would still hold water, but figured it was by the street because the owners were throwing it away. Hannah grabbed it and headed home.

She found Jamie and Wes playing hopscotch in the courtyard. She plopped down the pool and opened the backpack. "No hot dogs, but ta-da!"

"Wow, Hannah! You must have made a lot of money on your paintings!" Wes said.

Jamie clapped his hands. "Berries! Yum! And a pool? Oh boy!"

Hannah felt her face getting hot. "I didn't actually sell them." She explained to Jamie and Wes how things didn't quite go as planned, and how she found another way to exchange her paintings for food.

"Good thinking, Hannah!" Wes said, reaching into the bag.

"The pool was next to the street and it has a crack in it. I think they were throwing it away, so I just took it. We need to watch them when they get home tonight, though, to see if they get mad," Hannah said. "If they look mad, I need to take everything back."

"Except for the berries," Jamie said.

"And these three potatoes," Wes said.

"And this tomato," Hannah added, laughing. "We're having this with our last peanut butter sandwich."

After lunch, Wes set up the pool in the freshly cleared area of the courtyard. After a few trips to the alley faucet with the bucket, they had enough water to wash away a lot of dirt and grime. Before long, the pool water was so dirty it looked like it had been filled from the river. Wes ran for one more bucket of water so they could rinse the soap out of their hair.

"Brrrr! That's cold. Once we get the fire pit built, we can warm the rinsing water," Hannah said.

When they knew it was about time for the neighbors to be home, the three children went to their lookout window to watch their favorite TV show—Mr. and Mrs. Pool, as they called them. Wes gave a play-by-play.

"Mrs. Pool just came outside. She has a clothes

basket with her and is taking clothes off the line. Mr. Pool just came outside, too. Mrs. Pool is talking to him. Oh! She found your paintings, Hannah!" Wes' voice quickened. "She's showing them to Mr. Pool. They turned them over so they've seen your note. They're walking to the garden. They're looking around the yard and looking over the fence and…whoa." Wes suddenly darted away from the window. "They're looking over here."

"Give me those," Hannah said. She creeped to the side of the window and slowly lifted the binoculars. "Mrs. Pool took the paintings inside the house."

"Well, that's a good sign," Wes said. "At least they didn't just tear them up and throw them away."

"It could be a good sign." Hannah looked hopeful. "But they wouldn't throw them away outside. Anyway, maybe she's saving them to show to the police."

Jamie gulped. "Did they seem mad?"

"No," Wes said.

They set aside the binoculars to have dinner. Hannah decided it would be okay if they ate more of the vegetables from the Pool garden, since Mr. and Mrs. Pool didn't throw a fit or yell or anything. They had fresh cucumber and sliced tomatoes with berries for dessert.

A welcome change from beans and peanut butter.

While Hannah enjoyed the fresh goods from the garden, she mentally planned the sketches she would make of her favorite parts of the yard. But her daydreams were suddenly cut short as a siren pierced the quiet of the evening.

"Oh no!" Jamie said, running for the window. "They called the police!"

12

THE BIG ADVENTURE

Exactly what Hannah was thinking. *Please don't stop here!*

The siren was getting louder, closer. It seemed to be coming straight toward them.

"Jamie, they wouldn't call the police because a few vegetables were missing from their garden," Wes said.

"There they go!" Jamie shouted. "It's a police car and 'ambalance'!"

"And they definitely wouldn't call an ambulance," Wes added.

"They just drove right past us," Hannah said, with relief. And they did, but then they stopped, and not very far away. "Let's go check out the other windows."

They ran to the west wing where they had a view of The Wheel and Deal. They could see the flashing lights, but they were on the other side of the building.

"Let's run over there to see what's happening!" Jamie said.

"No, Jamie. We would just get in the way and we

might be recognized. Let's clean up our dishes and then we'll read, okay?"

"Ok," Jamie said. "Would you read your Nancy Drew book to me?"

"Sure! Do you want to listen, too, Wes?" Hannah grinned.

"Ha ha ha. I'll read my own book, thanks."

They read until bedtime and slept through the night.

At breakfast, Hannah suggested an idea for the day. "I think we have the courtyard area cleared enough of weeds that we could build our fire pit. Should we work on that today? Once we get it finished, we could cook some green beans and potatoes."

"Yeah, let's do," Wes agreed. "It's getting cooler at night, so a campfire would be great."

They got busy right after breakfast. They each grabbed an empty tin can to scoop out dirt where they would place the pit. When the bottom was a nice bowl shape and just the right size, they started placing stones in the bottom.

"Why do we need stones in the bottom, Hannah?" Jamie asked. "Dirt won't catch on fire, will it?"

"No, but the stones help hold the heat so our meals will cook faster. It looks nice, too," Hannah answered.

They finished lining the bottom with stones, then stacked larger ones around the rim. "Let me get the grill rack to see if this will work," Wes said. He retrieved the rack from the wagon and laid it over the stones. "We need the stones a little bit closer." They rearranged the stones until the rack sat level.

"Perfect!" Hannah declared.

They spent the rest of the day building a brick path around their yard. They took a break for lunch, but then continued to work on it after. Jamie was more interested in playing on the patio, but Hannah and Wes kept at it. It would take them several days to complete since they only had tin cans to use as shovels, but Hannah was pleased with their progress.

Covered in dirt and tired of working, they filled the pool and soaked.

"Ah. I don't mind that the water is cold today," Hannah said.

"Me either," said Jamie. "It feels good."

That night, they built a fire and roasted potatoes,

carrots and baby onions.

"That was yummy!" Jamie declared.

"It *was* good, wasn't it? Too bad we only have the green beans left," Hannah said.

"There are plenty of vegetables left in the garden," Wes said. "Give me a couple more paintings and I will go back tomorrow when they are at work."

"We'll all go," Hannah said. "I love their yard and I want to see it again."

"Me too," said Jamie. "I can help you pick berries."

"Eat them, you mean," Wes said. "Ok, we'll watch for them to leave in the morning and then we'll all go."

Hannah hopped right up the next morning, eager for the day's adventure. They hurried through breakfast and quickly washed up. Hannah pretended to herself she was being allowed to go to a friend's house to play—Annie's house—even though she wouldn't be there. Still, it was something different for them to do and the anticipation was building.

Wes watched out the window through his binoculars. "Mr. Pool is leaving now."

"Ok, let's take the bucket instead of the back-pack this time," Hannah said. "The veggies can be a little messy. I think I'll take the butterfly painting and the river scene. I'll write 'thank you' on the back of the butterfly and I'll tell her the bigger one is for the pool and tell her I hope it was okay to take it."

"Ok and now Mrs. Pool is gone, too," Wes said. "Ready guys?"

"Ok," Jamie said, clutching Lion and Blankie.

"Jamie, you need to help us pick and carry. Leave Lion here. Why would you take Blankie, anyway? Do you plan on taking on a nap while we work?" Hannah teased.

"If we go to jail I want Lion and Blankie with me."

Hannah felt bad. "Jamie, you're not going to jail! None of us are. I know it seems like we're stealing, but we're trading. Instead of paying with money, we are paying with paintings. When we get more sketching paper, I will paint them more pictures to pay them back, okay? I think you should leave your friends here so you can carry back more berries."

"Ok. But can we give them this rock, too? I'm pretty sure it's gold." Jamie was holding up his favorite glittery rock that he found by the river.

"Sure. That's gotta be worth a lot of berries."

Hannah was worried that she was setting a bad example for Jamie. *No, you're keeping him from going hungry,* she decided.

Hannah led the way down the alley in a direction Wes and Jamie had never gone before. She turned left onto a narrow sidewalk that led to the street one block east—the street that ran in front of the Pool house. They walked through their front yard and into the back along the privacy fence that separated the Pool's yard from Mr. Crane's.

Hannah smiled as soon as she stepped into the

Pool's backyard again. To her it was a wonderland and she never wanted to leave. The grass was cushiony—not like Olga's bare and bumpy yard. She buried her nose into the sheets billowing on the clothesline. *How wonderful it would be to sleep with a sheet...especially one that smelled like this.* She pinned her paintings next to them making sure they were upright and easy to find. Just beyond were the blackberry bushes, so overgrown you could barely see the supporting trellis beneath.

Jamie had found them right away. "Mmmm. Berries," he said.

"Be gentle when you pick them and put them in here," Hannah said, handing Jamie a washed-out bean can. "Put more in the can than in your mouth or you might get a belly-ache."

"Okay, okay."

With Wes and Jamie there to help her, Hannah took her time exploring the garden. There were flowering shrubs, colorful trees and flower beds full of autumn colors—burnt sienna, cadmium orange and pale sage green. Hannah tried to memorize the scene so she could paint it later.

She finally directed her focus on the vegetable garden, in raised beds of weed-free rows. "Who knew food could look so pretty," she said to nobody in particular.

"I've got more onions and carrots, Hannah. Where did you find the potatoes?" Wes asked.

"They have to be dug up. I'll do that. Why don't you pick some more tomatoes?"

Hannah took off her shoes and socks so she could feel the cool grass. She ignored the vegetables for a minute while she skipped up and down the length of garden. Then, to make sure she remembered how, she finished with a cartwheel. "Look, Wes! It's a hummingbird! Over by the sundial. Remember when Mom put out hummingbird feeders? She said they always showed up the first of May and stopped coming the first of October."

"I remember," Wes said. "I guess they'll only be here a few more days."

Hannah put her shoes back on, grabbed the shovel and dug up more potatoes. She decided to skip the beans. There weren't many left on the plants and they still had some from the last picking.

Wes had picked several tomatoes and held them up in outstretched hands. "Do you think this is enough, Hannah? I want to leave them some. Hannah?"

When Hannah didn't answer, or even look his way, Wes followed her gaze. Jamie wasn't at the blackberry bushes anymore. He was standing at the privacy fence, looking up at the man staring back at him. "Hi, Mr. Crane." Jamie greeted him like a long lost friend.

"Mr. Crane? That's not my name. What are you doing there, son?" As though the big purplish smile and stained teeth didn't tell him exactly what Jamie was doing.

"Oh, I'm just picking some berries. See?" Jamie tilted his bean can to show Mr. Crane the three berries rattling around the can.

"Jamie, hush," Hannah said, as she scurried to the fence. "We're just, I mean, uh… we're the gardeners, sir! Just pulling some weeds and removing some of the spoiled vegetables." Hannah made the motions of looking around the yard. "Yep. Looks pretty good now, so we'll be leaving. Just need to put our tools away. Sorry if we disturbed you. Have a nice day." Hannah hoped Mr. Crane couldn't hear her heart pounding in her chest.

"You're mighty young gardeners, aren't you?" Mr. Crane asked.

Jamie giggled. "Yeah. I'm five and Wes is— ".

"Jamie!" Hannah interrupted, trying to pull Jamie away from the fence. "It's time to go."

Jamie wasn't quite ready. "What *is* your name, Mr. Crane?" Jamie asked, as Hannah pulled with a little more force.

"Wait!" Jamie yelled, twisting free. "The gold!" He ran back to the blackberry bush and placed the rock gently beneath, then waved over his shoulder to the ever-watchful Mr. Crane.

"My name is Clipper, Curtis Clipper," he responded.

13

TRADING AT THE WHEEL AND DEAL

"Jamie, why are you laughing?" Hannah failed to see the humor in getting caught.

"Didn't you hear him? His name is Clipper! Get it? Toe-nail clipper?" Jamie erupted in another round of laughter.

Wes snorted, trying not to laugh.

Hannah wasn't buying it. "Oh, Jamie. You're making that up."

"No. I promise. He said 'my name is Clipper, Curtis Clipper.' "

Now Hannah smiled. "Ok, but that was a close call. If we ever go back, we have to be very quiet. NO TALKING."

Hannah couldn't bear the thought of not going back. They had only left the yard minutes ago, but she knew that even if she had to go alone, she would return.

"And speaking of funny, Jamie Faris, you should see your face! How many berries did you eat?"

Jamie smiled wide, showing off his purple teeth. He looked in the can. "I saved some for you guys. Hannah can have two and Wes can have one or Wes can have two and Hannah can have one."

Hannah laughed. "Oh brother! Thank you very much for your generosity!"

"We didn't get as much food as last time, but we have enough for now," Wes said.

That evening, Wes announced when the Pools returned home. Hannah and Jamie rushed to the window. They watched them go into the backyard and directly to the clothesline. Mrs. Pool took both paintings off the clothesline and turned them over.

"I think she smiled," Wes said, watching through the binoculars.

"Really? Or are you just saying that?" Hannah asked.

"No. I think she smiled. It's hard to tell from this far, but I think so," Wes answered.

Hannah's smile suddenly disappeared. "I wonder if Mr. Clipper will tell them about us."

"What's wrong with that? They already know we took their vegetables," Wes asked.

"It's just that SOMEBODY was blabbing our

names and ages all over the place in front of Mr. Clipper!" Hannah responded.

"Oh yeah? Who kept yelling 'Jamie this' and 'Jamie that'? Anyway, Mr. Clipper's no tattle-tale," Jamie offered, defending his new friend.

After dinner, Wes helped Jamie with his schoolwork. Hannah worked on a sketch of the hummingbird in the Pool's backyard.

"I need to get some more sketch paper," Hannah said. "I have one sheet of paper left."

"That won't be easy to find," Wes said.

"I know. I've been thinking that we need to get some warmer clothes, too. I'll take our extra set of summer clothes with me to the Wheel and Deal tomorrow to see what I can get. Maybe they would let me trade my art for a sketchbook, if they have one around."

"Pretty soon we're going to need more blankets, too. It's been getting a lot colder at night. Too bad this building doesn't have a fire place," Wes said.

The next morning after breakfast, Hannah stacked the summer clothing she had washed out. She added some watercolor to the sketch she had made of the hummingbird. She added a flower and the sundial to the picture, as well. As soon as it was dry, she signed her initials and tucked it into the sketchbook. She stacked their library books on top of the sketchbook until it was time to go.

"Ok. The sketch is all flattened now. Jamie is coming with me to the Wheel and Deal, Wes. Do you want to go, too?"

"Not unless you need me. I was going to gather up some firewood for our next campfire and then work on the brick path."

"Ok. We'll help you when we get back."

Hannah proceeded with caution to the Wheel and Deal, but there was no sign of Olga's car and not very many customers inside the shop. Fortunately, she didn't recognize any of them. She relaxed and let Jamie wander while she searched for clothes.

She found a large selection of clothing in their sizes, so it was just a matter of picking out what each would like. Wes was easy—a sweatshirt and jeans. She found some corduroys for Jamie. Those would keep him extra warm. She found a long sleeve cotton t-shirt and a pull-over sweater to match. That would be good for him to put on when they were sitting around the fire at night.

Now for herself. Her jeans and her bib overalls

still fit her fine, but she needed a long sleeve shirt or sweatshirt. As Hannah lifted the stack of clothing, she spotted a pale green sweater with violet flowers. It was soft and so pretty. *Was she being silly to want to wear something so pretty?* She decided to keep her eyes open for something warmer while she looked for socks.

That's about the time she heard Jamie blurt out, "What in the Sam Hill!"

Hannah whipped her head around. "Jamie!" And then she saw what Jamie had seen—their one-of-a-kind glow-globe. And not just their globe but their mother's easel and a basketball that looked a lot like Wes'—deflated from sitting unused for so long. She walked across the aisle for a closer look. There was her old Barbie doll she got for her seventh birthday. She knew it was hers because her Barbie could only wear one shoe. The other foot was flattened from Jamie using it as a chew toy. Wes's rock collection was there with both halves of the geode Dad had hammered open for him. *But how did this stuff get...?*

Hannah and Jamie looked at each other. *Aunt Ogre had been here!*

"May I help you?" One of the ladies that worked in the store had just walked up. Hannah thought she looked familiar, though she hadn't waited on Hannah before. *Maybe she looked like one of her teachers? Or someone on TV?* She had a friendly smile and kind eyes.

Hannah couldn't help but smile back. "Oh, hi," she responded.

"That's my glow-globe!" Jamie said, interrupting Hannah to point out their belongings "And that's Hannah's—."

"Oh, uh, he means he li-likes that globe," Hannah said.

"Well, duh, Hannah. I like it because it's mine!" Jamie insisted.

"Jamie, shush!"

The lady looked at the globe and back to them with an odd expression. "Oh dear. I remember the lady that brought it in—along with several other things. She was about my height, but a little bigger. She had dark hair and these bun things on the side of her head." The lady held up her pointer fingers at the side of her head and made spiral motions. "She traded them for a couple of porcelain cats. Does she sound familiar?"

"See, Hannah? It was the ogre."

Hannah laughed nervously. "She does sound like an ogre." She quickly stepped between Jamie and the clerk, giving Jamie a meaningful glare before turning her back on him.

Jamie peeked around Hannah and looked up at her. "*The* Ogre, Hannah."

"Ma'am, I was wondering if we could trade these summer clothes I brought in for these warmer clothes I've picked out. I was just looking for one more sweater. Oh, also, do you have any art paper? Would you accept a painting in exchange for paper?"

"First of all, you don't need to call me ma'am. My name is JoAnn," she said with a big smile. "You can call me JoAnn or Mrs. Wheel, whichever you prefer. Now let's take these up to the counter and you can show me the painting. Is it an original or a print? Oh, I see you have a sketchbook there. It must be original."

"Yes, it's an original ma'am. I mean, Mrs. Wheel."

Hannah gave Jamie one more threatening look as they followed JoAnn to the counter.

"Quit squinting at me, Hannah. You don't scare me."

Hannah bent down to get into Jamie's face. "Quit using my name!" she hissed.

Jamie squinted back, whispering, "Hannah Hannah Hannah."

Hannah placed her sketchbook on top of the counter, but before she could open it up, Jamie was dashing back down the aisle, "I'll be right back. I'm just going to get the glow-globe."

Hannah twisted around and knocked the sketchbook behind the counter in the process. "Oh, I'm sorry, Mrs. Wheel. I need to go get him."

"Of course, dear. And pick out the sweater that you want, too." Mrs. Wheel retrieved the sketchbook from the floor and placed it back on the counter.

Hannah returned with the pretty sweater and a red-faced Jamie, squirming to get away from her tight grip. A little out of breath, she opened the sketchbook and pulled out the hummingbird painting. "I know it isn't much, but if I could get more paper, I could make you others."

Hannah was shy about showing people her art. If she saw Mrs. Wheel smile, she would know that she liked it. But when Hannah looked up, Mrs. Wheel wasn't smiling. Hannah felt her cheeks grow warm. *Oh no, she doesn't like it!*

Mrs. Wheel stared at the painting as though frozen. She slowly looked up at Hannah, then at Jamie, then back at Hannah. "Are you 'hlf'?" JoAnn asked, pointing to the initials on the lower right-hand side of the painting.

"Yes."

JoAnn nodded, and looked back down at the painting. When she looked up again, her eyes were shimmery. "It's just lovely, dear."

Hannah could have dropped to the floor; she was so relieved. "Oh, thank you, Mrs. Wheel." *She must really like hummingbirds.*

Mrs. Wheel looked uncomfortable. She made a fist with her right hand and gently tapped the counter. Then, speaking softly, "I think I know...I mean, would you allow...oh dear." She stopped and looked up at Hannah.

"Is everything okay, Mrs. Wheel?" *So, she likes it but it isn't enough.* "I know it's a small painting, but if I had more paper…"

"No, no, I'm fine. It's fine. These clothes will certainly do for the ones you picked out and I think I may have some art paper in the warehouse. I will need to look through some boxes, though. Could you come back? Let's see. This is Wednesday. Tomorrow may be too soon, but could you come back on Friday? Do you live far?" JoAnn asked.

Jamie pointed across the street. "We live over there at Horse…"

"Hold these!" Hannah handed the stack of clothes to Jamie—covering his mouth with them.

"We live close, Mrs. Wheel. I will come back Friday. Thank you for the clothes!" She picked up her sketchbook and pulled Jamie quickly out the door.

14

TROUBLE TROUBLE TROUBLE

Jamie dug in his heels. "But, Hannah, what about my globe?"

Hannah silently pulled on Jamie's arm until they were across the street and out of earshot of Mrs. Wheel.

"Jamie! What is wrong with you? We can't let anyone know who we are or where we are living! Don't you get that by now? Do you *want* to go back to Olga's?"

"No! You're hurting my arm, Hannah."

Hannah released him. "You practically told Mrs. Wheel everything about us! I'm surprised you didn't invite her for dinner!"

"Oh yeah. *Come over for a cracker and some beans, Mrs. Wheel.* I'm not stupid, Hannah." By this time, Jamie had tears streaming down his face. When he got to the third floor and saw Wes, he ran to him sobbing.

"Jamie! Are you ok?" Wes checked him for an injury, then looked up at Hannah. "What happened?"

It was Jamie who answered. "Hannah is being mean to me just because I wanted to get my glow-globe out of the Wheel and Deal and just because Mrs. Wheel wanted to know if we lived close and she was really nice so I wanted to tell her, but no! Then Hannah squinted at me real mean and yelled at me and so now we have to go back to Olga 'cause I've ruined everything!" Once Jamie took a breath, the sobbing got louder. Then he started to cough.

"Calm down, Jamie. I'm sorry I yelled," Hannah pulled Jamie to her and gave him a long hug. "It's okay." But it was then she heard a sound like tearing paper in his chest. Jamie tried to wiggle free, but she held on to him.

"Jamie, take a deep breath and let me listen." It was definitely coming from his chest. The sound was alarming. She held him back at arm's length. "Do you feel okay?" Hannah asked.

"No." Jamie gulped. "I'm sad."

"Can you breath okay?" Hannah asked.

Jamie shrugged. "Most of the time, except when I..." He started to cough again. When he finally caught his breath, he answered, "cough."

"Ok, you need to rest. I'll get you a drink of water," Hannah said.

Hannah had noticed him coughing off and on, but figured it was just a tickle in his throat, probably from thirst. This was more serious and she would have to keep an eye on him. Once he was settled, Hannah filled in the gaps of the thrift shop experience for Wes.

"All of our stuff was there, Wes. But Mrs. Wheel was really nice. I'll go back Friday to see if she found some art paper."

"Me too. I'll help you, Hannah," Jamie offered.

"No!" Wes and Hannah answered in unison.

"I think it's a good sign that Aunt Ogre took our stuff to the Wheel and Deal, don't you?" Wes asked. "If she was going to keep hunting for us then she wouldn't have done that, right?"

"I don't know. Maybe she thought this would be a good punishment for us. Oh, and she traded them for more cats, if you can believe it!"

"Maybe she was just feeling the need for more lifeless cats staring at her," Wes said. "But what if she finds us, drags us back and then we have even less than we had before?"

"Then we leave again, that's what," Hannah said.

Hannah put Jamie to bed early that night, hoping sleep would help his cough, but his breathing sounded bad even while he slept.

"I don't think Jamie should go to the library tomorrow. The walk up the hill could tire him out too much, but I want to get on the computer and research his cough. I don't know if it's a cold or something worse. It keeps coming back."

"Ok. I'll stay here with him while you go," Wes offered.

But when they told Jamie the next morning, he had other ideas. "What do you mean stay home? I have been thinking about the *libary* every day. I finished all my books and I want to pick out some new ones."

"I'll get some for you, Jamie," Hannah said. "I don't think it would be good for you to do all that walking when your cough has come back."

"I want to pick out my own books! You're just mad at me about yesterday and you want to punish me like Olga does so you're going to make me stay inside!"

"Jamie! How can you say that? I want you to stay here and rest because I'm worried about you." Hannah was hurt that he would think otherwise.

"What if I pull him up the hill in the wagon, Hannah?" Wes offered.

"Yeah, what about that, Hannah?" Jamie chimed in. "I probably just need some fresh air."

And so it was decided. They finished their breakfast, brushed their teeth and gathered their books for the library. Wes pulled the wagon out from under the loading dock. Hannah folded up the blanket into the right size to pad the bottom of the wagon for Jamie. He settled inside with Lion by his side, happy with his new mode of transportation.

Hannah carried the books while Wes pulled the wagon. As they got to the second hill, she could see Wes was struggling. She put the books in the wagon with Jamie and helped Wes pull. "At least it's downhill on the way home," she said. "Are you getting another book, Wes?"

"Yeah, I'm going to see if there is a sequel to Hatchet. Oh, wait. Did you want to read it before I return it?" Jamie answered.

"That's okay. I'll check it out sometime later. I'm still in the mood for more Nancy Drew, but I guess you liked it if you're looking for a sequel," Hannah said.

"Yeah. It was really good. It was about a boy trying to survive in the wild on his own." Wes looked at Hannah and smiled.

When they reached the library, Jamie seemed no worse for wear—just coughing occasionally—though Hannah and Wes had to stop and catch their breath.

"Ok, first I'm going to help Jamie look for books,

then I'll grab the next Nancy Drew. When you're done, come and watch Jamie so I can do that computer research I mentioned."

"Ok, see you in a few," Wes answered.

But then something strange happened. The librarians were quite used to seeing the children come in on a regular basis and had always been friendly—until now. They looked right at the children, but before the children could smile and wave, they hurriedly looked down again. They appeared to be looking at something on the desk as they whispered to each other. They glanced at the children again, then down.

Jamie didn't seem to notice. He gave his usual jovial greeting to the two, "Good morning, *libarians*," but their response was guarded. One slowly raised a hand as though thinking about waving, but then lowered her gaze.

That's weird, Hannah thought. She looked back at Wes to see if he had noticed. He looked at Hannah and shrugged. *He had seen it, too.* Hannah saw him go out of his way to get a peek at the paper on the desk. He looked back at Hannah with an odd expression.

Jamie got busy searching through picture books. If he had a particular animal on his mind, he would zip through the aisles in search of that animal. Today he was grabbing a number of zebra books. She let him pick out whatever he wanted this time. She glanced across to where Wes had gone. She spotted him at the computer across the way.

"I'm done, Hannah! I found all these zebras and a cool book about planets, see? I bet Wes doesn't know everything inside this one. Let's go get your Nancy Drew book," Jamie said. "Can I pick out the next one?"

"I think I'll get two this time. Let's look for 'The Clue of the Leaning Chimney' and 'The Secret of the Wooden Lady'."

"Ok. Thanks for the clues!" Jamie ran for the junior fiction section of the library.

"Walk," Hannah called out then froze in her tracks when a familiar face popped out between the rows of bookshelves.

"Hannah?" Annie said.

Hannah could feel her heart racing. She needed to run, but before she could move she was wrapped up in a bear hug like only Annie could give.

"Annie!" Hannah could feel her eyes start to water.

"Hannah. You're so thin! Are you ok? We've all

been so worried about you," Annie said.

"Oh," Hannah giggled nervously. "We're fine, Annie. We just…wait. Why aren't you in school now?"

Annie looked over her shoulder and pointed to a group of students Hannah recognized. "We're here with Miss Brown. Most of the class is over by the fire place getting free hot chocolate. But, Hannah, why aren't *you* in school? We thought something happened to you. You stopped coming to school and then your aunt was…"

"We go to a different school now," Hannah blurted. "They start later, but we're going to be late, so I need to hurry." Hannah turned to look for Jamie.

"But Hannah…," Annie said.

Hannah spotted Jamie coming toward her. "I'm sorry, Annie. I'm sorry I couldn't tell you good-bye but I miss you. I miss you a lot!"

"But what school do you go to now, Hannah?" Annie said.

By then, Jamie was in ear shot. "Oh, hi, Annie! We don't go to school anymore 'cause we…"

"Jamie!" Hannah laughed nervously. "Brothers!" She took the books from Jamie and pulled him away from Annie as fast as she could. As she headed toward the computers to find Wes, she nearly knocked him flat.

He looked at her with alarm in his eyes. "We need to leave now! Follow me!"

"Because of the students?" Hannah asked.

"No! The police!" he whispered. "He's talking to the librarians, but he's here for us!" Wes looked scared as he led them in a zigzag path through bookshelves and worktables toward the exit. He stopped them behind the last row of books. There was one way into the library and one way out. A big, wide corridor led from the librarians station to the doors. They couldn't get to the doors without being seen.

"Oh no," Hannah whispered. "I haven't checked out the books yet."

"There's no time!" Wes said, looking back at the front desk. "They're distracted. Run!"

They ran to the exit and almost made it out undetected, but a piercing alarm sounded before they got the big double doors open.

Jamie stopped to cover his ears. "That means someone's stealing books!" he yelled.

"We are!" Wes said. "Hurry!"

They ran out the door. Wes lifted Jamie and plopped him in the wagon. Hannah wedged the books in beside Jamie. "Let's go!" she called. She had seen the policeman when the alarm sounded, and knew he could easily outrun three kids and a wagon.

Wes and Hannah both had a grip on the wagon handle, but going downhill with two of them pulling was awkward and a little bit dangerous.

"Slower on this corner," Wes warned. "Hang on, Jamie!" They eased up around the corner and ran for the alley. Another bumpy, brick alley.

Hannah looked behind her. Nobody seemed to be following and Jamie was really getting bounced around. "In here," she said, leading them into hidden steps behind the nearby church.

Hannah and Wes were gasping for air. Jamie coughed.

"Are you okay, Jamie?" she asked.

"Can we go slower?" he asked, loosening his grip on the wagon.

Hannah peeked over the partial wall. "Nobody in sight. Let's go, but we'll go slower." She picked up the books and let Wes pull the wagon.

Further down the alley they encountered a dumpster. "Stop behind there," Wes said. They hid behind the dumpster and listened. Nobody was coming.

This time they didn't stop until they got inside Horseshoe Hideout. Once inside, they all collapsed.

"Weird that the policeman didn't follow us," Wes said, finally able to talk.

"Oh my gosh! I can't believe we're book thieves now!" Hannah said. "Why do you say the policeman was there for us, Wes?"

"I saw the librarians acting strange and pointing to something on the desk."

"Yeah, I saw that, too," Hannah said.

"It was a newspaper, so I looked it up on the computer. We're on the front page. The headline said 'Have You Seen These Children'. Below it was our school pictures from a couple years ago."

"I wasn't in school a couple years ago," Jamie said.

"I know, bud. You weren't pictured," Wes said.

"Huh? That's not fair." Jamie missed the point.

"They probably had to use old ones since Olga doesn't pay for us to get our school pictures taken. They wouldn't have one of you."

"Well, I guess they aren't looking for *me* then." Jamie said.

"Did the article say Olga is looking for us?" Hannah asked.

"I didn't get that far. I saw the headline and the pictures and then ran to get you guys. And we didn't steal the books, Hannah. We'll return them to the drop box when we're done reading them. When you're done reading them. I didn't even get one and I guess I won't be able to now. We can forget ever going back."

Hannah sagged to the floor, disheartened at the truth of his words. "There's another reason we can't go back."

Wes looked at her, waiting.

"Annie saw me."

"She was there?" Wes asked.

"Yes. Miss Brown's English class was there, but Annie was the only one that saw me, I think."

Hannah repeated their conversation to Wes. "At least, I think that's what we said. I was so nervous, I can't be sure."

"But please can we still go back?" Jamie begged. "The *libary* is my favorite. The river and the libary are."

"Not if they're looking for us there, Jamie. In fact, anyone that saw the newspaper could be looking for us. Sorry you didn't get a book, Wes," Hannah said. "If it makes you feel any better, I got two Nancy Drew books this time. I'll share."

"Oh boy," Wes answered.

"Oh no. I didn't get a chance to research Jamie's cough, either," Hannah said. "I wanted to see what we can do to make it go away."

They took the steps slowly to their third-floor room. Hannah didn't want to start Jamie coughing again. He looked pretty worn out.

Jaime picked up the canteen and shook it. "I'm thirsty, but this is empty. Is there any water in the jug?"

"Oh no. We forgot water, too," Hannah said. "What else can go wrong?"

"I'll get some from the alley," Wes offered.

"Do you think you should go right now after what just happened?" Hannah asked.

"We need water, especially after all that running.

Just keep watch for me. It'll be fine."

Once Wes was out the door, Hannah pried open a window overlooking the street.

"Do you think Aunt Ogre told the newspaper about us?" Jamie asked.

"I don't know, Jamie. If she was going to do that, I think she would have done it when we first..." Hannah suddenly stopped talking.

"What's wrong?" Jamie asked.

Hannah raised the window higher. She started making strange noises.

"What are you doing, Hannah?" Jamie asked. "Are you seeing how far you can spit?" Jamie looked out the window and saw a truck pull onto the property.

"Hannah whistle!" Jamie urged. "Whistle like a bob-white, Hannah. Wes needs to know there's a truck here."

But Hannah continued making strange noises.

"Is your whistler stuck?"

Hannah nodded, panic in her eyes.

Jamie watched the alley entrance. As soon as he saw Wes he stuck his head out the window and began to yell, "BOB-WHITE, BOB-BOB-WHITE," followed by a round of coughing.

Wes looked up. Jamie and Hannah waved him back. He ducked back into the alley.

Hannah ran to the windows over-looking the loading platform. The truck was pulling a short trailer. It stopped, the driver got out, unhitched the trailer, then got back in his truck and drove away.

"It's gone now." Hannah sighed in relief.

"Wes is coming back," Jamie said, still watching from the far windows.

Hannah ran to Jamie and gave him a hug. "Oh, Jamie. Thanks for remembering the song."

"That's okay, Hannah." Jamie gently patted her back. "I'll teach you how to whistle again when I learn."

Hannah met Wes at the top of the stairs. "I'm sorry, Wes. I tried to whistle, but I panicked. Nothing would come out."

"That's okay. I heard Jamie loud and clear."

"It was almost a whistle, wasn't it?" Jamie asked.

"Almost, bud!" Wes ruffled Jamie's hair.

"Did you see what the trailer said?" Hannah

asked. "Wheel Construction Inc."

"Another Wheel," Wes said. "I wonder if they're related?"

"What's construction ink, anyway?" Jamie asked.

"'Inc' means it's a business," Hannah said. "'Construction' means it's a building business. They're going to be working here, like we thought. The trailer probably has the tools they need to put on the shingles."

A portable outhouse, building material and now a trailer. Hannah sensed that their days at Horseshoe Hideout would soon be coming to an end. The world was closing in on Hannah and her brothers; specifically Aunt Ogre, the librarians, the police and the Wheels. Even running into her very best friend seemed more like a threat than a comfort. The more people closing in on them, the more alone Hannah felt.

It really was just the three of them against the world.

15

UNWANTED IMPROVEMENTS

The next morning, the children scraped together a light breakfast. They ate slowly to make it last.

"Drink more water," Hannah offered. "It will help you fill up."

A large rumbling sound came from outside. They ran to the window. Another truck—this one delivering a garbage dumpster.

"We should probably stay inside today. And away from the windows," Hannah said.

It was a wise decision. Within the hour, workers swarmed the property. They assembled scaffolding to go up the side of the building. Then they laid boards across the supports on the scaffolding. They climbed all the way to the roof. Before long, a loud scraping could be heard from above. Shingles flew past the window and into the dumpster below. Workers down on the ground picked up any scraps that didn't make it into the dumpster and tossed them in.

The children tried to pass the time with schoolwork and checkers, but it was hard to focus.

At lunch time, they realized the commotion had stopped.

"They must have gone to lunch," Hannah said. They all ran to the window. "Yep, they're gone."

"Quick. Let's hit the outhouse while we can," Wes said.

"What are we having for lunch? I'm hungry." Jamie asked.

"We have one can of pork and beans, a few crackers and a tomato," Hannah said. "We can share half for now and half for dinner. We should hunt for worms as soon as the workmen leave. If we don't catch a fish we may have to…"

Wes interrupted before she could finish her thought. "Hannah, I'm going back to the garden. I know you don't have any paintings left to trade, but I'll leave them a note that I will pay them back when I can. When you get more art paper, you can make them more pictures."

"We don't even have paper to write a note," Hannah answered.

"We saved the cherry pie wrappers. I'll write on

the back of one of those," Wes suggested.

Hannah was too hungry and too tired of beans to argue. She was also upset that they couldn't return to the library ever again and that she didn't know what was wrong with Jamie. Being trapped inside to wait for the workers to leave reminded her too much of living with Olga. She let Wes go without another word.

Wes wrote out a note, slipped it in his pocket and left with the bucket for vegetables and an empty can for berries.

As much as Hannah wanted to go back to the garden, she didn't want to leave Jamie and he wasn't well enough to try to outrun the workmen. Wes alone might be able to find a way to sneak back in unnoticed.

She opened the last can of beans and sliced the tomato. She laid out their plates with two crackers each, two spoons of beans and a slice from the tomato. *It really wasn't that bad of a meal, when you considered what th ogre allowed them to eat.* She read some Nancy Drew to Jamie while they waited for Wes.

Suddenly, the barn door slid open and slammed shut. "I'm back!" Wes shouted from below. He took the stairs faster than usual.

He sounds happy, Hannah thought. There must

have been some potatoes left in the garden.

When Wes appeared at the top of the stairs, he had a big grin on his face. "Ho Ho Ho! Merry Christmas!" He held up the bucket and a small cooler Hannah had never seen before.

"A cooler? How?" was all she could say.

"Check this out. First I got these from the garden." Wes lifted the bucket with assorted vegetables. "The berries were pretty much gone, so I didn't get any, but then I left the note on the clothesline and look what I found." Wes pulled a piece of paper out of his pocket and put it on the table.

Hannah read it aloud for Jamie.

Dear Children,

There is a small cooler by the patio door. We put ice in it so everything will be fresh, but use the milk and hot dogs before the ice melts. When you are done bring back the cooler and we'll get you more. Help yourself to the garden and don't forget the apple tree!
Youʼre welcome!

Hannah and Wes stared at each other in disbelief. Jamie clapped his hands.

"Oh my gosh! It *is* like Christmas. And an apple tree?" Hannah asked. "How did we miss that?"

"I don't know but it was full of apples, so I got some of those, too."

"Milk and hot dogs!" Jamie lifted the lid on the cooler and pulled everything out. "Look at this. A whole package of hot dogs. One, two, three, four, five, six, seven, eight hot dogs. And peanut butter and bread. Hey, potato chips! What are these?"

"They look like homemade muffins," Hannah said. She opened the wrapping. "Mmmm. Apple."

"And three cartons of milk," Jamie added. "We'll never be hungry again!"

They were all so happy to have milk with their meal, they didn't mind the beans. They split an apple and each ate a muffin to celebrate.

"After the workers go home tonight, lets roast the hot dogs, Hannah," Wes said.

"I hope they go home early!" Hannah said.

"We can each have two hot dogs and we'll have two left over. I want potato chips with mine," Jamie said.

And that's what they did. After the workers went home for the day, Wes whittled sticks into skewers for the hot dogs. Hannah built a fire in the new fire pit in their courtyard. Jamie played a slow game of hopscotch, frequently stopping to rest.

When the hot dogs were done, they each ate one wrapped in a slice of bread and shared a bag of chips.

"This is sooooo good. I don't even miss having mustard or relish," Hannah said.

"Mmmhmm," Wes responded with his mouth full. "or ketchup."

"Or chocolate cake and ice cream," Jamie added.

They all laughed.

"So the Pools aren't mad at us for taking their vegetables or they wouldn't have given us all this food," Hannah said.

"Nope. I think they know we're hungry and they want to help," Wes said.

"That's really nice of them. But if they find where we're living, they'll still have to turn us in and give us back to Ogre." Hannah said.

"I guess. And what about the workmen?" Wes

said. "I watched one of them climbing the ladder past our windows and he stopped and looked in at our things. We're bound to be found out if we stay here much longer. It's not too fun being trapped inside again."

Jamie was busy redrawing the lines on his hopscotch squares.

Wes used a stick to pick up the grill and poke at the fire.

Hannah watched the embers cool. "We've been lucky so far, but I guess you're right. We should start looking for a cave by the river. It's just that I think a fire inside the cave will make Jamie's cough worse."

"We can't have a fire inside the cave, Hannah. We could get carbon monoxide poisoning and die," Wes said. "We could try to keep one going outside the cave. But, I don't know. I mean, we're out of food. Maybe we should go back to Ogre's house. That way we could go to school again, too."

Hannah rested her head on her knees. "I miss school, too, Wes, but I don't miss being Olga's prisoners and punching bags. I can't stand the thought of her hitting Jamie again. You know she is going to be so much worse if we go back. Jamie is happy now. Ok, Jamie is almost always happy, but we're mostly happy, too, aren't we?"

"Yeah. I don't want to go back to Ogre's house, it's just that I miss school and I miss the library and there won't be any gardens to ransack once it snows. I doubt if the Pools want to feed us all winter."

Hannah's shoulders slumped with the weight of it all. She picked up a stick and started making doodles in the dirt.

"And I really need to get my hands on the next Nancy Drew," Wes added.

Hannah gave him a quizzical look. "What?" Hannah sat up, grinning. "You read them? And you liked them! Thought so."

"Ok, you win. I liked them. You don't need to rub it in, though."

"I'm not going to rub it in. Hey, Jamie! Guess who else likes Nancy Drew mysteries?"

Jamie plopped down between Hannah and Wes. "All of us! I bet if Nancy were real, she'd be looking for us, wouldn't she? We're the big mystery now."

"Maybe. If she were real and she lived in Flinthills," Hannah said.

They watched the fire slowly burn down as the sky darkened around them.

"Wow. Look at the stars!" Jamie said.

"They're really bright tonight," Wes said. "Look, there's Orion's belt."

"Where?" Jamie asked.

Wes pointed in the western sky. "See those three stars in a row? Follow my finger all the way up."

"Oh yeah. Show me the big dipper again, Wes."

Wes showed Jamie the big dipper and how to use the north star to find the little dipper. "The big and little dippers make a full circle around the north star every day, just like riders on a Ferris Wheel. Did you know that?"

"They do? Wow! Wouldn't that be a fun ride!" Jamie said.

16

MR. AND MRS. POOL

The ice was still in the cooler the next morning so they ate three more hot dogs that they had cooked the night before.

"I don't want any bread with mine," Jamie said.

"Me either. Cold dogs are better without, huh?" Wes agreed.

They used the outhouse and fetched water before the workmen arrived.

"We can share the last two hot dogs for lunch and then I'll take the cooler back," Wes said.

"As long as the workmen are gone," Hannah said. "I'm supposed to go back to the Wheel and Deal today to see if Mrs. Wheel found any art paper. I'll have to wait until the workmen go home, though. I hope she'll still be open."

The workmen did leave at noon, so Wes returned the cooler with a cherry pie wrapper thank-you enclosed.

They stayed inside the remainder of the day waiting for the workmen to leave.

Jamie didn't seem very interested in Hannah's suggestions for their entertainment that day. Even Nancy Drew failed to hold his interest.

"Hey, I've been thinking up new slogans for the Flinthills broom company. How do you like this one? 'You can ride them or hang them or push them on the floor. Come to Flinthills Broomery to shop in our store'."

She was sure that would make Jamie laugh, but he barely smiled.

"No? How about this one? 'Need new brooms for your witchery? Fly on over to Flinthills Broomery'. Not sure that really rhymes."

"It doesn't," Jamie said.

"What's wrong, bud?" she asked.

Jamie only shrugged.

Hannah reached out to fluff his hair. She pulled her hand back quickly, as though she'd been scorched. "Jamie! You're burning up!"

Wes put down the carving he was working on and rushed over. "Do you hurt somewhere?"

Jamie shrugged. "Sometimes it hurts here," Jamie pointed to his chest. "Mostly, I'm just tired."

Hannah opened the sleeping bag and had Jamie lie down. She covered him with the blanket and got him a cup of water. "Here, drink this." She held his head while he took a sip. "I should have gone back to the library. We need some kind of medicine or…I know. We need to put a cool washcloth on his forehead."

Wes jumped up to get one. When he had it moistened he handed it to Hannah. She dabbed it on Jamie's forehead. "I think I can make a disguise and get back into the library," Hannah said.

"Do you want me to go?" Wes asked.

"No, you don't have any way to disguise yourself. I can pull my hair back and cover it up in a kerchief or a hat. Stay here with Jamie. Hold this on his forehead. When the washcloth gets warm, wet it again and put it back on. Keep doing that. And have him drink more water.

"The workmen are gone now, so I'm going to run over to the Wheel and Deal before they close. I'll be right back. I'm sure they have something I can use to cover my hair. Keep drinking the water, Jamie, and try to rest, okay?"

"K." He curled into a ball and closed his eyes.

Hannah ran down the stairs and across the street,

tears burning her eyes. *What should I do? He needs a doctor. How do I get him to a doctor? What if I'm caught at the library?* She stopped outside the door of the Wheel and Deal, took a deep breath trying to compose herself. She wiped her eyes and walked in.

Mrs. Wheel stood behind the counter. She smiled and waved when she saw Hannah. "Oh, hello, Hannah! I was afraid you wouldn't be able to make it today. I think you'll like what I found."

Hannah winced at the sound of her name, but of course she would know it. Jamie used it freely when they were here last. Hannah felt tears well up in her eyes thinking about Jamie again—how mean she had been to him that day. *Don't start crying. Not now.*

Hannah looked down at the counter, stunned at what she saw. A new sketchbook, a package of real watercolor paper, a box of crayons, a coloring book, three tablets and a box of pencils. Everything looked brand new—never opened.

"You *found* all this?" Hannah asked in disbelief. "It all looks brand new, Mrs. Wheel."

"Is it what you wanted, dear?" Mrs. Wheel had a hopeful look on her face.

"It's so much more. Who would trade all this

away?" Hannah asked.

"Oh, I don't remember, but it's yours. I'm happy to help you, Hannah. *Anyway* I can." She said that last bit very slowly, the smile no longer on her face.

Oh no. Hannah could feel her nose redden and her eyes fill. *Don't cry don't cry don't cry.* She didn't dare look up. She just stared at the art supplies waiting for them to come back into focus. Before she had time to recover, Hannah felt Mrs. Wheel put her hand over her own. *Oh no. She's being too nice.*

Mrs. Wheel picked up a piece of paper and placed it where Hannah could see it. Even through the tears, Hannah recognized it, because she had drawn it—the sketch of Olga that she had meant to destroy.

Hannah wiped her eyes and looked up. "How did you…?" She stopped when she saw tears in Mrs. Wheel's eyes.

"It fell out of your sketchbook when you dropped it Wednesday. When I saw it, I recognized the woman right away. This is the woman that brought in your brother's globe, the one he calls 'the Ogre'." She squeezed Hannah's hand. "She must have been very cruel to you and your brothers. Hannah, would you let me help you?"

The kindness was too much. Hannah bit her lip, willing the tears to stop, but it was no use. Her feelings gushed out with her tears. "I just want the three of us to be safe and to be together. I want someone kind to take care of us, but if you tell the police that you found us, they'll make us go back to her or they'll split us up."

Mrs. Wheel came around from behind the counter and hugged Hannah. Hannah remembered being held like this when she was younger and how it made her feel safe. She closed her eyes and let herself be held.

Mrs. Wheel released her from the hug, but held her by her shoulders. "Hannah, my husband and I have always wanted children—three, in fact. You would make us very happy if you would come to live with us."

Hannah stared at Mrs. Wheel. *Did she really just say that?* "You want us to live with you? All three of us?"

"Yes, dear. I spoke to my husband about this as soon as I saw your picture in the paper, before I knew you were the ones leaving the art on our clothesline..."

"What?" Hannah took a step back. "You're Mrs. Pool?"

It was Mrs. Wheel's turn to look puzzled. "Mrs. Pool?"

"We call you Mr. and Mrs. Pool because we took your pool. I'm sorry about that, and the vegetables. No wonder you looked familiar to me." Hannah sniffed and wiped her eyes.

"Oh nonsense," Mrs. Wheel said, waving her hand in the air. "I'm glad you took them. But, Hannah, what do you think about living with us? We would like to give you a real home. A safe home."

"But is that even allowed? What about Olga? Our Aunt Olga? Don't we have to go back to her now that you know who we are?" Hannah asked.

"She is never going to bother you again, dear. She is not allowed near you or your brothers."

"My brothers! Jamie!" Hannah exclaimed.

"Yes, Jamie, too. Your other brother is Wesley, right? That's what the paper said."

"Oh, Mrs. Wheel! Jamie has a fever and a cough. He says his chest hurts. I think he's really bad. Can you help us?"

"Oh goodness! That poor little guy. Let me call Robert and I'll have him meet us over there."

"Over there? You know where we're living?" Hannah asked.

Mrs. Wheel patted Hannah's hand. "It didn't take us long to figure that out, but we'll fill you in on all that after we get Jamie to the doctor, okay? Let me call Robert and we'll drive over to get the boys. Oh, and dear, why don't you call me JoAnn?"

Hannah knew she wasn't dreaming, because she had never allowed herself to dream anything so wonderful. But she wouldn't let her mind wonder on everything this could mean for them. She had to focus on one thing.

Jamie had to get better.

17

THE HIDEOUT REVEALED

Hannah felt weird being driven to the hideout. Weirder still, getting out of the car in broad daylight without having to hide.

Hannah looked up at the third floor window. She figured Wes would have heard the vehicle and the doors shutting. He was there, watching. She couldn't make out the expression on his face, but she was sure he was surprised. She waved to him, to let him know it was okay. He waved back.

"Oh, there's Robert now," JoAnn said. A tall, pleasant looking man rushed toward them. *Yes, that's Mr. Pool.*

"Hannah, I'm so glad to finally meet you," Robert squeezed her shoulder. "I called Dr. Schack on the way here. He'll get us right in. Let's go get your brothers, shall we?"

Wes stood at the top of the stairs—his eyes the size of saucers. Hannah was pleased that she was about to give him the best news of his life.

"Wes, this is Mr. and Mrs. Pool, I mean Wheel. Mr. and Mrs. Wheel. Uh, Robert and JoAnn. They're going to take Jamie to the doctor and they said…" Hannah took a deep breath to try to control her voice, but her lip refused to stop quivering. "They said we could live with them." Wes looked at her like she had a third eye.

Robert held out his hand for Wes to shake. "Wes, I'm Robert. I'm happy to meet you, son, and I'm anxious to get to know you better. What Hannah says is true, but we need to get your brother to the doctor as quick as we can. Is he—?"

"This way," Wes scurried into their third-floor campsite where Jamie was lying on the sleeping bag.

He was awake now and slowly sat up to study the visitors. "Well, what in the Sam Hill are you doing here, Mrs. Wheel?"

"Jamie," Hannah warned.

Robert and JoAnn couldn't help but chuckle.

"Hi, Jamie. Why don't you call me, JoAnn, sweetie." She knelt down on the sleeping bag and touched Jamie's forehead. "Jamie, this is my husband, Robert. He's going to carry you downstairs and then we'll take you to see a nice doctor—Dr. Schack. He's a friend of ours and he's going to help you feel better, okay?"

"K. Can Lion go, too?"

Hannah grabbed his stuffed lion. "I'll carry Lion

and you carry Blankie, ok?" She picked up Blankie and handed it to him.

"Ready?" Robert asked. "Here we go, Jamie." He bent down and swept Jamie up into his arms.

Jamie smiled all the way up. "Do that again."

Robert smiled. "As soon as we get you better, kiddo."

JoAnn took Wes by the hand. "I'm so happy to finally meet you, Wes. I want to thank you for coming into our backyard."

Wes smiled. "It was Hannah's idea, but you're welcome."

JoAnn kept up a steady chatter while they drove to the doctor. She told them about their three bedroom house with plenty of room for all of them. One of the rooms has twin beds so the boys can share that room and Hannah can have her own. Since she and Robert have been foster-parents for years their meeting with Child Protective Services went very well. That's what she and Robert were doing the day before, which is why she wanted Hannah to come back to the shop on Friday, not Thursday.

"So everything is all set and you can come home

with us as soon as Jamie is done at the doctor. Mrs. Stapp from Child Protective Services is coming over tomorrow to talk to all of us together. It is just a formality. They want to make sure you are okay being with us and so forth."

Wes looked over the top of Jamie's head at Hannah while JoAnn continued to jabber. Hannah smiled at him and Wes smiled back. He reached over to Jamie and ruffled his hair. Jamie smiled at Wes, then lay his head on Hannah's shoulder.

Jamie had a bronchial infection. The doctor gave him medicine for the fever and the infection. He said that when Jamie was all better, they would run some tests on him to see if he may have asthma. That could explain why his cough would come back frequently, but it would be difficult to diagnose while he was ill. The doctor said they should call him at home if Jamie got worse, but he expected him to start improving immediately.

"No running and jumping for a few days, Jamie. Rest and drink plenty of fluids, okay?"

"K," Jamie said.

Hannah was so relieved that Jamie was expected to get well so fast.

"Thank you, Dr. Schack," she said.

"You're welcome, Hannah. You did the right thing asking Bob and JoAnn to bring him in. Bronchial infections can easily lead to pneumonia and that can be quite serious."

Before they got back into the car, Hannah ran to JoAnn. She wanted to give her a hug, but felt shy. "Thank you for saving my brother."

"I'm sure it wasn't easy to trust a stranger, Hannah. You were very brave to let me know Jamie needed help. Now let's get you all home and settled in."

They got in the car and headed for home—their new home.

"Will you tell us about Olga, JoAnn?" Hannah asked.

"Shhhh, Hannah," Jamie said.

"She knows about her, Jamie. She said we don't need to worry about her anymore."

"We don't?" Jamie asked in surprise.

"That's right. You don't," JoAnn said. "The very day she brought your things into the thrift shop, she got into a car accident—right outside the shop. They said she was eating fast food while she was driving and spilled something on her lap, causing her to swerve. She drove right into a telephone pole. She was injured and had to go to the hospital, but she's out now.

"The police were involved, of course, and they had been working on a warrant to search Olga's house so it all wrapped up very quickly after that."

"Why did they want to search her house?" Hannah asked.

"For you three! Your school was concerned that something had happened to you. A Mrs. Lippert called Olga asking about you. Olga lied and told her that you were all sick. When you didn't return by the start of the following week, Mrs. Lippert called again. Olga told her you were still sick. Mrs. Lippert wanted her to take you all to see a doctor, but Olga told her to mind her own business. Mrs. Lippert told her that your welfare was her business. She said she was bringing homework to you that night and she was bringing the school nurse with her. Olga never answered the door and she didn't answer any more phone calls from the school.

"So the school went to the police. The police got Mrs. Stapp involved. She couldn't get Olga to co-operate either so that's why the warrant."

"I saw our pictures in the newspaper," Wes said. "I guess it wasn't Olga that was looking for us."

"No, it wasn't. Olga wouldn't even cooperate with

the police…at first. They searched her home, but didn't find any evidence of you children ever being there. They went back to the hospital and put more pressure on Olga. They told her that they suspected her of murder! That loosened her tongue, finally. She told the police that you had run away the first part of September and she never reported you missing. I don't know if she ever looked for you."

"We think she was looking for us the day after we left," Hannah said.

"We saw her drive by our hideout looking around," Wes added. "She even got out of her car and looked in our direction."

"Until a bug bit her and she smacked herself in the face!" Jamie laughed until he coughed.

"Oh! I bet that was fun to see," JoAnn said.

"Yeah, but we think she was really just looking for her can opener and cherry pies," Jamie added.

They all laughed.

"Well, they put that story in the paper once they got a confession from her. I suppose there is a chance she'll go to jail, but her lawyer is working on a plea. She might just get probation and community service. Either way, she's not allowed to come anywhere near you three.

There is a court order to keep her away."

"She was very mean to us," Hannah said. "I don't think the community is going to want her service."

"I think you may be right about that, Hannah. I don't see a woman like that feeding the homeless. Maybe they could have her pick up trash along the highway, or something like that." JoAnn said.

"She has bad bunions, so that won't work," Jamie offered. "Better just haul her away."

Robert snorted. JoAnn whipped her head around to the front of the car, covering her mouth.

"JoAnn, how did you know we were staying at Horseshoe Hideout?" Hannah asked.

"Horseshoe Hideout?" Robert asked.

"Oh, that's what we call the building. There's a horseshoe hanging from the big sliding door. Jamie said it brought us good luck, so he gave it that name."

"It did, Hannah," Jamie insisted. "It got us out of the rain when we ran away and it brought us the blue bathroom so we wouldn't have to go behind a fire hydrant and it brought us fish from the river and vegetables and a pool and now it brought us Mr. and Mrs. Pool even though they're really Mr. and Mrs. Wheel. Robert and JoAnn."

Robert chuckled. "Well! When you put it that way, it does sound lucky. And we were lucky to find each other when we did. We're doing some major renovations on that building. It wouldn't have been safe for you to be there, not to mention it was probably getting pretty cold at night, wasn't it?"

"Yes," Wes said. "But Hannah was going to draw more pictures to trade for blankets."

"Anyway, one of the roofers spotted the wading pool and campfire in the courtyard below. When we went down to investigate, it was obvious that someone had done a lot of work cleaning up the area. There was evidence of a recent fire and someone had been playing hopscotch." Robert glanced over his shoulder, smiling. "Anybody you know?"

"I guess we weren't being as careful as we thought," Hannah smiled back.

"I'm glad you were close enough for us to keep an eye on you," Robert said.

"And what a shame if you had been so careful that we would never meet," JoAnn added. "I don't want to think about that."

"What will Horseshoe Hideout be after the renovations?" Wes asked.

"The lower floors will be shops and offices and the third floor will be our new home," Robert said, as he pulled the car into the driveway. "Once you get settled inside, I'll show you the plans we have drawn up. We might need to make some revisions to include that horseshoe hideout idea, though. I like it."

"You're going to live on the third floor?" Jamie said. "That's our floor!"

Robert shut off the car and turned in his seat. "We hope it will be your floor again when we move in next year, Jamie. We want you to be our family and go with us wherever we go," he explained.

Jamie looked at Hannah and Wes with an expression of utter delight. "You guys. They want us to stay." Jamie couldn't believe it. "Wait. All three of us, right?"

"All three of you," Robert said, chuckling.

Hannah lay her head against the back of the seat, closed her eyes, and smiled.

Safe and together.

18

WANTED

Robert and JoAnn gave the children a quick tour of their home.

"Oh my gosh! This is so beautiful. Why do you want to move from here?" Hannah asked.

"This has been a nice home for us, but Robert has had his eye on your hideout for years. He has a nice space designed and I have wanted to open a bakery for years. That will be one of the shops on the first floor. The lot behind is very large so we can have an even bigger garden and not just one apple tree, but a little orchard. *And*, it will have four bedrooms so you will each have your own room. Wasn't that good planning?" JoAnn winked at Hannah.

"Now how would you children like to soak in a bubble bath or take a shower while we fix dinner? We have one bathroom around the corner there, and then there are two more upstairs. We can go shopping for some new clothes tomorrow, but I can find you some t-shirts to wear for now," JoAnn offered.

"A shower sounds great, but we have clean clothes at the hideout. I forgot to bring them," Hannah said.

"Oh good. Robert can run over there and get your things while I start dinner."

"Do hamburgers sound okay?"

"Mmmm. That sounds so good," Hannah answered, her stomach growling in response.

"Any ideas what you'd like to have with your hamburgers?"

The children all looked at each other, but remained silent.

"Come on. Don't be shy," JoAnn urged.

So they all shouted at the same time:

"Baked potato!"

"Cole slaw!"

"Chocolate cake and ice cream!"

Robert and JoAnn laughed.

"Whoa. You've really thought about this, haven't you?" JoAnn said. "I might have to come up with some substitutions for tonight, but tomorrow night we'll have all of those things. How does that sound?"

"Perfect," Hannah said.

"Mrs. JoAnn, er, JoAnn, can we use a little hot

water in our bath?" Jaime asked.

"Of course you can. I mean, I would hope that you would." JoAnn had a puzzled look on her face.

"Olga wouldn't let us use any," Wes explained.

"Oh good heavens. That woman." JoAnn looked up at her husband, shaking her head.

"Use all the hot water you need," Robert assured them. "I'm going to start the grill for the hamburgers and then run over and get your things from the hideout. I'll be back before you're done with your showers."

He was back with time to spare. The children used all the hot water they needed and then all the hot water they wanted, until it was gone. When the water in her shower started to get cool, Hannah shut it off, fearful that something had broken. She dried off, dressed and went downstairs to share her concern.

Robert and JoAnn were in the kitchen fixing dinner. "How was the shower, Hannah?" Robert asked.

"It was really good, but I think something broke. The water started to get cold."

Robert laughed. "I guess we should have warned you that three of you bathing at the same time—and for over thirty minutes—would likely drain the hot water heater. But don't worry, it will fill back up soon. You didn't break anything."

Wes and Jamie soon joined them in the kitchen.

"This is the cleanest I have *ever* been in my whole life," Jamie exclaimed. "I'm so clean, I'm wrinkled."

They all laughed. "That hot water will probably be good for your cough, too," JoAnn said.

"Mmmm. Something smells really good," Jamie said.

"Dinner is ready, so let's eat!" Robert said.

They sat down to a real family meal. They had hamburgers, French fries *with* ketchup, and a salad. The children were mostly quiet while they savored every bite.

"We have strawberry shortcake for dessert, if you have room," JoAnn said.

"Oh no. That sounds good but I'm stuffed," Hannah said, holding her stomach. "That's more food than we've eaten in a long time."

"I'm stuffed, too," Wes agreed. "And it was the best meal I ever remember."

"Maybe just a little bit of dessert for me," Jamie

said.

When dinner was over, they carried their dishes to the kitchen, prepared to wash their own.

"Now you just go sit down and rest. Robert and I will clean these up tonight. Check out the bookshelves in the living room to see if there is something you may want to read or you can watch TV."

"TV, yeah! Where do you keep your binoculars?" Jamie asked.

Hannah laughed. "They mean real TV, Jamie."

Robert showed them how to turn on the TV and find a station they would like. By the time he and JoAnn had cleaned up the dishes, the three were asleep on the sofa.

"Poor things are just exhausted," JoAnn said. "Well, let's get them up so they can sleep in beds tonight."

Wes and Jamie shared the room with the twin beds, and Hannah got the third room to herself. Being on a bed again felt like a luxury to Hannah. She closed her eyes and felt them burn with unshed tears as she recounted the events of the day. It started with such worry and despair and now this. For the first time since arriving in the Wheel home, she allowed herself to think of what life might be for them now.

They can finally return to school. They can see their friends and teachers again. She can apologize to Annie for not being honest with her. Maybe she could finally go to her house. Maybe Annie could come over to Robert and JoAnn's house. They will have running water, good food and real indoor bathrooms—but she may need to shorten her showers. She hoped to be able to return the library books and be forgiven so she could keep her card. No more running and no more hiding. Best of all, they'll have Robert and JoAnn to look after them. At last, Hannah fell into a deep and restful sleep—that lasted for nearly an hour.

It was the shaking that woke her up. Jamie shaking her shoulder. She opened her eyes to see Wes, Jamie and Lion staring at her.

She sat up immediately, and for a second, forgot where she was. "What's wrong?"

"He can't sleep," Wes said. "He wants us all together. I'm too tired to argue."

"Ok. Hop up here, bud."

And that's where JoAnn and Robert found them in the morning.

"He'll get used to it. He just needs a little time," Hannah suggested. "He's been sleeping next to me and Wes for two years."

They ate breakfast—cereal with milk and berries—no measuring, no limits. After breakfast JoAnn suggested a shopping trip.

"Robert said he brought all your belongings from the hideout, but there just weren't many clothes at all. You'll be going back to school on Monday and you'll want to look your best. So, new clothes and shoes, I think. It's getting cooler so we'll get jackets, too. We can worry about heavier coats a little later in the season."

"School!" Jamie shouted. "Yes! I can't wait!"

They were all excited to be going back to school.

"Can we go to our same school?" Hannah asked.

"Yes, dear," JoAnn said. "I think Mrs. Lippert would come and pick you up herself if it was necessary, just to make sure you did. I can drop you off before work, so that's no problem.

"Mrs. Stapp will be here this afternoon. We should take care of the shopping this morning so we're back in time to have lunch before she arrives."

Hannah was eager to go shopping, but the boys

wanted to stay with Robert.

"Hannah knows what we like. She can shop for us," Wes said.

Hannah didn't mind. It felt a little strange going somewhere without her brothers, but she knew they were in good hands with Robert.

The last time Hannah had been shopping for new clothes was with her mother. When she and JoAnn stepped into the first shop, Hannah had a feeling similar to when the three of them returned to the river bank for the first time. She was flooded with wonderful memories, but sad at the same time. This time was different, though. It's true that her mother was not there with her, but she wasn't alone. She was sharing the experience with another kind and generous woman that cared about her. Hannah knew her mother would like JoAnn and would want Hannah to be happy.

And Hannah was happy. With JoAnn's help she picked out school outfits, everyday clothes, pajamas, under clothes, new shoes, and jackets for herself and her brothers.

Midway through their shopping, they took a short break. They stopped into a coffee shop where Hannah had her first cup of hot chocolate in years—complete with a mound of whipped cream. She was having a nice time, but something was troubling her.

"JoAnn, I have to tell you something," she began. *She deserves to know that we're more than garden robbers.*

"What is it, Hannah?"

"I stole books from the library."

JoAnn chuckled. "Oh, I know about that, dear. This whole town has been worried about you children as soon as news spread about Olga's accident. The librarians and the policeman just wanted to see you safe. They know you didn't mean to take those books."

"Then why didn't they come after us when we ran out and set off the alarm?" Hannah said.

"They were afraid that if they chased you, you might get away from them and leave Flinthills for good. As soon as Robert and I figured out who you were, we called the police and convinced them to let us approach you. If you hadn't come back to the shop Friday, Robert and I were going to come to you at your hideout. We can take the books to the library later today and have them officially checked out. Will that make you feel better?"

"Oh, yes, it would. Thank you." Hannah relaxed and then confided more to JoAnn. "We knew we had to leave the hideout. We knew we couldn't hide from the workers much longer. We were going to find a cave to live in, but then Jamie got sick."

"Well, I'm sorry he got sick, but maybe that's what it took for you to realize you needed help." JoAnn put her hand over Hannah's. "Now, let's drink up so we can finish our shopping, shall we? You have enough clothes for now, but I think we should pick out some school supplies."

By the time they finished, they had the back seat of the car and the trunk crammed with packages. Hannah smiled to herself admiring all the colors filling the back seat. She couldn't wait to dress for school Monday.

"Whew! Wasn't that fun?" JoAnn asked.

"So fun. Thanks, JoAnn," Hannah answered.

When they returned home, Wes and Jamie helped with the packages, both interrupting the other to tell Hannah about their day.

"Robert is a fisherman, Hannah!" Jamie said.

"And he has a boat!" Wes added. "Can you believe it? I told him about our trips to the river and digging for worms and cooking our catch."

"And I told him about my flying sunfish," Jamie added.

Robert came out to help carry packages, too. "These kids love the outdoors, JoAnn. The weatherman says we're going to have a nice day tomorrow. Maybe we should pack a picnic and take a boat ride after breakfast. See if anything is biting."

"I like that plan," JoAnn said, smiling.

"Boys, you want to help me get the gear ready? We'll need to pick up some lifejackets, too."

"Sure," Wes said. "Can we take Dad's pole with us when we go?"

"Of course. I put it in the garage, right next to the others."

Hannah and Jamie carried the boys packages to their room. She showed Jamie all his new clothes. He especially liked the safari shirt and the brand new shoes.

"Gee, Hannah. This is a lot of stuff. JoAnn's a lot nicer than Ogre, isn't she?"

"Yes. They are nothing alike, thankfully."

"Do you think Mom would like JoAnn?"

"I'm sure of it. She would want someone kind to take care of us. JoAnn reminds me of Mom."

"Good, because I really like her," Jamie said.

After the lunch dishes were cleaned up and put away, Mrs. Stapp came to the house. She visited with everyone together in the living room.

Hannah had butterflies in her stomach. She was nervous that there might be a lot of rules to follow or else they would be taken away from the Wheels. But it wasn't like that at all.

Mrs. Stapp was nice. She reminded the children that Olga was not allowed near them and what they were to do if they ever saw her near their school or their home. She explained what it meant to be in foster care, that Robert and JoAnn had fostered many children and they should feel safe living with them.

Hannah momentarily quit listening. Something about those words troubled her. The butterflies were back.

When Mrs. Stapp finished talking to them as a group, she asked to speak to Hannah alone. She told her how sorry she was that Hannah and her brothers had lost their parents. "And I'm so sorry that you spent the next two years living with such an uncaring woman. I wish I could have prevented you from going through that experience, Hannah."

"Olga told us if we complained, we would be put

in separate homes. I wanted us to be together, so we didn't tell anybody."

"Olga was wrong. We want families to stay together, too. I want you to remember that we are here to help you. I'm going to leave you my card and I want you to call if you ever have any questions or concerns. But I am sure you can tell by now that Robert and JoAnn are very caring people."

Hannah bit her lower lip. There was a question on her mind, but she feared the answer.

"What is it, Hannah?" Mrs. Stapp asked.

Hannah took a deep breath. "You said that Robert and JoAnn have had many foster children. Why aren't they still here? Didn't they want them to stay? Will we only be here for a little while?"

"Oh! No, not at all. Let's see, they watched twin babies once while the mother was hospitalized. The father was in the service overseas, so she really needed the help. They watched a young girl for a time while her mother was in…well, she was going to be gone for a few months. Eventually the grandparents brought the train from Florida to pick her up. Then there was the time the football team from Burlington was stranded when their bus got stuck in the snow. They had a house full of teen-age boys for a couple nights before the parents could all come and claim them.

"Robert and JoAnn have wanted children for a long time, but could never keep any that they sheltered. Until now. They want to adopt you and your brothers, Hannah. They told me that from the start. I hope that's what you want, too."

Hannah realized she'd been holding her breath.

"That's what I want, too."

19

RETURN TO HORSESHOE HIDEOUT

The children settled into a happy life with Robert and JoAnn. They were back to school and back in good standing at the library—not that they ever fell out of good standing. In fact, Wes and Jamie each got their own library card.

JoAnn arranged tutoring for Hannah and Wes to make sure they would not be left behind in their classes. On the other hand, they had done such a good job teaching Jamie, he was actually ahead of his class in many subjects. He was also the star at Show and Tell in his classroom with tales of his adventures as a runaway—always with a humorous twist.

Annie was so happy to have her friend back. She knew Hannah wasn't being honest with her at the library. "In case you didn't know it, you're a very bad liar, Hannah Lynn. So just don't even try it again."

Hannah laughed. "Gladly!"

Not only were the children reunited with friends, but they were allowed to take part in after-school activities and even go to friends' houses. They often had friends come to their house after school or for sleepovers on the weekend.

Jamie and Mr. Clipper became fast friends. Jamie confided in him that they had watched him clip his toenails one night and that's why Jamie thought his name was so funny. Mr. Clipper threw his head back and laughed when Jamie told him.

Jamie finally started sleeping in his own bed—all night. Hannah came up with the idea that they should retrieve the glow-globe from the thrift shop and put it on Jamie's nightstand. "Leave it turned on at night and he won't want to leave it," she suggested. She was right.

The children anxiously watched as Horseshoe Hideout transformed. After the new shingles and new windows and doors and after the brick work was all cleaned up, work started on the inside. It wasn't as easy to watch the progress inside, but every now and then Robert would take them over to do a walk-through after the crew had left.

The entire third floor would be their home. There would be offices on the second floor and shops on the ground floor. Hannah was most excited about the new shops. Well, Jamie was very excited about the bakery that JoAnn would be opening, but there was also to be a flower shop, an art supply store and a combination bookstore and coffee shop called Horseshoe Hideout.

When the last bit of touch-up paint had been

applied and the landscaping all done, Robert brought JoAnn and the children over for the big reveal.

"We can take the stairs or the elevator," Robert offered.

"Elevator, Poppa Bob," Jamie decided, using his new pet name for Robert.

When the doors opened, they were in a wide-open entry looking into a beautiful living room where their table, bench and sleeping bags had once been. The children ran to the windows and stood in awe. They could see the river, just like before, but now through new, clean glass. A telescope was perched by the window so they could watch boats and barges drifting by or point it to the sky for stargazing.

Next to this room was a wide-open kitchen and dining area. All the surfaces were shiny and bright, but what caught their eye was the glass doors at the end of the room—where there once were windows overlooking their courtyard. Robert opened the doors onto a little balcony and guided them out.

They had a bird's-eye view of a most magical courtyard complete with a small pond and fountain, winding brick paths and a stone fireplace. The old patio was still there, but it had a new tile surface, a table and chair, and a big shade umbrella attached to the table. The rickety fence had been replaced with a tall stone fence and gate. The old rusty horseshoe had been welded right into the center of the wrought-iron gate.

"Wow," Hannah said. "I love the flowers and twinkle lights and the fountain."

"But no baths in the fountain, Jamie," JoAnn added.

"No way, Momma Jo. I only bathe in hot water now," Jamie said.

"Can we cook-out in the fireplace?" Wes asked.

"And roast marshmallows?" Jamie added.

"I hope we do. That's why it's there," Robert said.

"Let's go look at your rooms now," JoAnn said.

The bedrooms were all along the west wing. Jamie's room was closest to Robert and JoAnn's.

"Wow! Look at that! My walls are the same color as Lion!"

He had bunk beds with a built-in tent and a desk with plenty of school supplies.

"When we move over, your globe can sit on your

desk right here," Robert said.

The wall opposite his bed had a huge map of the world and a well-stocked bookcase. Another wall was a magnetic blackboard.

"You can use it to practice your letters or to color," JoAnn explained. "You can stick these magnets on it, too. See?"

Jamie excitedly took it all in. "We can play school, Hannah!"

"It'll be fun playing school here. This is perfect," Hannah said.

"And you can camp in your own tent every night," Wes added.

Jamie hugged Robert and JoAnn. "Thank you Poppa Bob, Momma Jo. I love my new room."

"We're glad you like it, Jamie," Robert said. "Let's check out your brother's room."

Wes stepped into his sky-blue room, trying to take in everything at once. His jaw dropped when he looked up. "I have a window in my ceiling?"

"I know how you like to be outside to look at the stars, so you can gaze at them from your own bed now, Wes," Robert said. "It's called a sky-light."

"My own telescope?" Wes asked in disbelief, noticing a telescope pointed toward the sky light.

"Do you like it?" Robert asked.

"I love it. I love it all," Wes noticed the bed with built-in bookshelves full of adventure stories and science books, a new desk with his rock collection and a new chess set. There was a large wicker basket full of sports equipment, including his old basketball. On the wall behind his bed was a huge map of the Mississippi River showing all the locks, dams, sloughs and islands near them.

"You can use that to help us navigate to the perfect sandbar," Robert said.

Wes smiled, nodded and then hugged the two people who cared enough to do all this for him.

Wes deserves a room this cool, Hannah thought, but she couldn't miss a chance to tease him. "Oh wait," she said looking through Wes' books. "There's something missing. There's no Nancy Drew in this collection."

"Real funny, Hannah," he said.

"Well, let's go see your room," JoAnn suggested. "He might find some there."

Hannah stepped into the garden that was her room. It was a beautiful shade of green, like a pale forest green with a touch of Caribbean blue. The white canopy bed was adorned in twinkle lights and a colorful quilt in patches of pale greens and pinks and violet—like a flower bed. The nightstand held a vase of fresh flowers in the same colors as the quilt.

"It's so beautiful," she said, her eyes darting around the room to take it all in.

She opened the closet door, amazed at the size. She too had a new desk. It had a built-in bookshelf with many volumes of Nancy Drew, as well as art books and even a diary. But what caught Hannah's attention and held it was the large worktable with open shelves full of artist paper, paints, pencils and paint brushes. A small wooden stool on wheels was tucked under the table, and right next to the table was the easel that had once belonged to her mother.

"It's everything I love. I never want to leave this room. Thank you so much," she said through her tears and hugs.

They moved in two days later. Only then did they notice that every room of the house featured a framed drawing by hlf: some of butterflies, some of flowers and one of her favorite fishing spot on the Mississippi.

The Faris children soon began thinking of Robert and JoAnn as their new parents, and the Wheels thought of the Faris children as their own. By the time they moved into their new home, the final steps toward adoption were nearly complete.

"We would love for you to call us Mom and Dad, but we know you have very fond memories of your real parents and we don't want to take anything away from that," JoAnn said, "so we will leave that up to you. Whatever you're comfortable with: Mom, Dad, Momma Jo, Poppa Bob or plain old JoAnn and Robert."

Robert continued. "But whatever you decide to call us, we need to put your last name on the final documents. Even though you will be our children, you are allowed to keep your last name of Faris, if that's what you prefer. We would love for you to take our last name, too, but another option you might prefer is to use both names and hyphenate them."

"Hyphenate?" Jamie asked. "Isn't that what a bear does in the winter?"

"That's hibernate, Jamie," Hannah said, starting to smile. "Hyphenate means you put a dash between two names and use them both."

Wes chuckled.

"So, if you decide to hyphenate your last name with ours, your new name would be Jamie Faris-Wheel," Robert explained.

Jamie's eyes were like saucers. "What? You mean like the Ferris wheel ride? And like how the big dipper and little dipper circle the north star?"

"Spelled a little differently, but yes," JoAnn said, smiling. "Though I didn't know that about the north star."

Jamie didn't hesitate. "Yes! I want that name!"

Wes nodded his head. "Me, too."

"We're in this together, so me three," Hannah said.

And so it would be. They were safe, they were together, and they could be children again—the Faris-Wheel children.

~The End...for now~

CPSIA information can be obtained
at www.ICGtesting.com
Printed in the USA
LVHW031324161220
674005LV00005BA/582